Daniel

at the

Siege of Boston
1776

✵

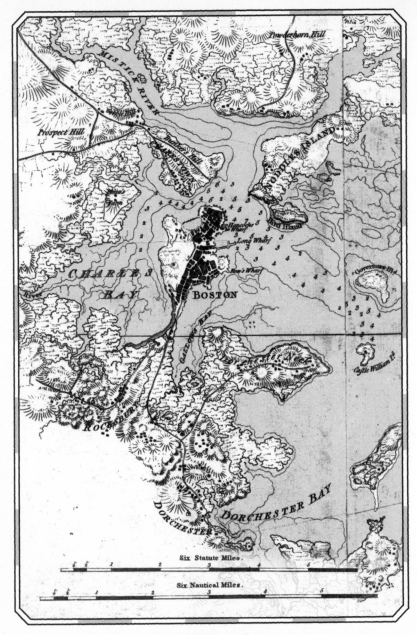

※ BOSTON BAY and VICINITY ※

Published according to Act of Parliament Nov 13, 1776

★ BOYS OF WARTIME ★

Daniel
at the
Siege of Boston
1776

LAURIE CALKHOVEN

DUTTON CHILDREN'S BOOKS

An imprint of Penguin Group (USA) Inc.

For my mother, with love and thanks

DUTTON CHILDREN'S BOOKS

A division of Penguin Young Readers Group

Published by the Penguin Group * Penguin Group (USA) Inc., 375 Hudson Street, New York, New York 10014, U.S.A. * Penguin Group (Canada), 90 Eglinton Avenue East, Suite 700, Toronto, Ontario M4P 2Y3, Canada (a division of Pearson Penguin Canada Inc.) * Penguin Books Ltd, 80 Strand, London WC2R 0RL, England * Penguin Ireland, 25 St Stephen's Green, Dublin 2, Ireland (a division of Penguin Books Ltd) * Penguin Group (Australia), 250 Camberwell Road, Camberwell, Victoria 3124, Australia (a division of Pearson Australia Group Pty Ltd) * Penguin Books India Pvt Ltd, 11 Community Centre, Panchsheel Park, New Delhi - 110 017, India * Penguin Group (NZ), 67 Apollo Drive, Rosedale, North Shore 0632, New Zealand (a division of Pearson New Zealand Ltd.) * Penguin Books (South Africa) (Pty) Ltd, 24 Sturdee Avenue, Rosebank, Johannesburg 2196, South Africa * Penguin Books Ltd, Registered Offices: 80 Strand, London WC2R 0RL, England

Although this is a work of fiction, many of the historical events portrayed and persons named are real. The author has used history as a stage for several fictitious characters, and any resemblance of those characters to actual people is unintentional.

"Boston Bay and Vicinity" and "Plan of the Town of Boston": Map reproduction courtesy of the Norman B. Leventhal Map Center at the Boston Public Library.

The publisher does not have any control over and does not assume any responsibility for author or third-party websites or their content.

CIP Data is available.

Published in the United States by Dutton Children's Books,
a division of Penguin Young Readers Group
345 Hudson Street, New York, New York 10014
www.penguin.com/youngreaders

Designed by Elizabeth Francis and Jason Henry
Printed in the United States * First Edition
ISBN 978-0-525-42144-3
1 3 5 7 9 10 2 6 4 2

siege [SEEJ] *noun* 1. The act of surrounding a city or town, cutting it off from food and other supplies, to force it to surrender.

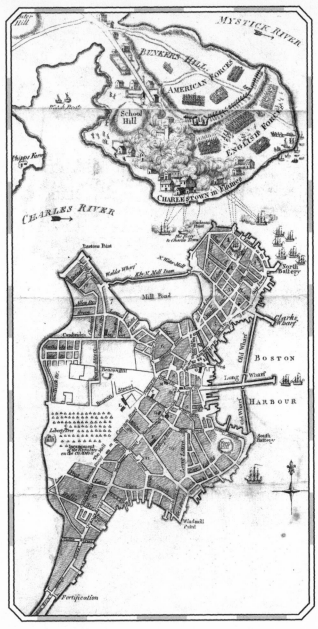

✳ PLAN *of the* TOWN *of* BOSTON ✳

with the attack on BUNKERS HILL *the* 17th *of* June 1775

★ CONTENTS ★

The Brink of War

T *he streets of Boston were crowded with British soldiers, sent by the king to show the rebels who was boss. Great Britain had tried to tax her American colonies, but the colonists objected. No taxation without representation!*

One night in Boston, an angry mob pelted nine British soldiers with snowballs and insults. The Redcoats leveled their muskets and opened fire. Five colonists were killed, including a former slave named Crispus Attucks and one seventeen-year-old boy. The event became known as the Boston Massacre. It was March 5, 1770.

After the massacre, most of the taxes were repealed. But Great Britain left one tax in place—a tax on tea.

In 1773 three tea-laden ships sailed into Boston Harbor.

Furious Patriots in Boston, known as the Sons of Liberty, vowed to prevent the tea from being unloaded. The governor of Massachusetts, loyal to the king, vowed that the tea would be unloaded.

The standoff lasted three weeks. Then the Sons of Liberty dressed up as Mohawk Indians and turned Boston Harbor into a teapot.

To punish the rebellious colony, an angry England once again sent soldiers to Boston. The harbor was forcefully closed and the British parliament passed a series of oppressive laws. The colonists found them intolerable.

With this punishment, King George thought he would stop the rebellion before it spread. But the Sons of Liberty had other ideas.

By the fifth anniversary of the Boston Massacre, the colonies were on the brink of war.

Daniel
at the
Siege of Boston
1776

✦

CHAPTER ONE

A Reason to Riot

March, 1775

I stared into Josiah Henshaw's red brown eyes and vowed not to blink. I had beaten him at too many games of ringer and had a pocket full of his marbles to prove it. Now he proposed a staring contest.

We were chest-to-chest, nose-to-nose, and I aimed to have the victory. His two eyes blended into one, the same color as my prized clay marble, my lucky shooter. I knuckled it for strength. Boys around us shouted encouragement.

His eyelids fluttered. I fought to keep mine open.

Then the bells fell to ringing, and I flinched. I blinked first.

"Hand it over, Daniel Prescott," Josiah cried. He shouted to be heard above the royal peal of Christ Church's eight bells, the sober chime of New North Meeting House, and the bells that rang over the rest of Boston.

His palm closed around my lucky shooter. It was a gift for my last birthday, my twelfth. There wasn't likely to be a present on my thirteenth in a few months' time. The British navy had blocked the harbor until the citizens of Boston agreed to pay for the English tea they had dumped into the water. The harbor was empty of merchant ships and the food and goods they carried. Instead, Boston Harbor was filled with the king's warships, and Boston's wharves were filled with British soldiers. They did not cut us off entirely. Other colonies sent us goods overland in wagons and carts. It was a long, difficult journey, and carts could not hold as much as ships. Food, and birthday gifts, were in short supply.

Josiah examined his prize with a sneer and fluffed the ruffles beneath his chin. "Father says General Gage will surely arrest the king's enemies today," he said. "What will you do if the liberty boys start a riot, Prescott? Hide under a pew?"

I wanted to knock his hat off, and his wig along with it. I turned from him without answering, ignoring the bold claims of the schoolmates who had gathered around our contest. Most shouted in support of Samuel Adams, John Hancock, Paul Revere, and the rest of the Sons of Liberty. A few, like Josiah, swore loyalty to King George like their fathers. I was careful, as always, not to state my allegiance to either side, to protect my father. But I didn't warm to being called a coward for it.

It was the sixth of March, 1775. Yesterday marked five years to the day since the Redcoats had broken the peace and shed the blood of Crispus Attucks and four others at the Boston Massacre.

I wondered what today's remembrance of the massacre would bring. Dr. Joseph Warren was to speak at Old South. I was one of ten from our school of two hundred and fifty selected to attend. Unfortunately, so was Josiah. Our schoolmaster had no choice but to include the son of one of the richest merchants in Boston.

Josiah said something under his breath to Ezekiel Partridge when Master Richardson joined us. I didn't have to catch Josiah's words. Our assistant schoolmaster's tattered shoes and worn coat had long been the subject of Josiah's ridicule. There were few of us who didn't suffer his mocking tongue.

I had a secret reason for wanting to be at Old

South. Josiah had led me to forget the task in front of me for a moment, but now the responsibility came rushing back.

"Lobsters," Timothy Otis muttered with disgust.

A company of Redcoats paraded to the beat of a drum, forcing us to move aside. Their black boots thumped against the cobblestones. I was used to their presence, but today fear rushed through me at the sight of them.

As we entered Queen Street, Master Richardson fell into step beside me. "Ready, Daniel?" he asked in a low tone.

I could only nod while my mind hurried over the details of my task. If I failed, the Redcoats would surely seize the men King George thought of as his enemies as Josiah had threatened. Today those men, including John Hancock, Samuel Adams, and Dr. Joseph Warren, would stand and defend our rights as Englishmen. And I would help them.

It was my duty to accost an ensign. Father and I had overheard the British plan to sabotage the Sons of Liberty the night before. Officers from the British Tenth Regiment had long ago made our tavern—Prescott's Tavern on Fish Street—their headquarters. They moved in believing Father to be a Loyalist to King George. We filled their tankards and their bellies, took their coin, and let them believe what they wished. They spoke freely and we gained valuable information for the Sons of Liberty.

Last night Father manned the tap and I helped serve the evening meal while we listened to Lieutenant Colonel Stockdale and his officers make a plan.

"When Warren's address becomes treasonous, we'll have a reason to arrest them all," Stockdale had said. "We can convince the governor to ship them back to England for trial."

"Surely Warren knows better than to speak treason in our presence?" one of the officers said.

Captain Smythe snorted. "What do these fool colonials know of matters of state?"

"No, he's right." Stockdale stabbed his fork into the fish pie I set before him. "Any arrest will set this Boston mob to rioting. Still, to have all of the leaders of the Sons of Liberty together in one place, and not seize them . . ." He sat thinking for a moment, then waved his tankard at me. "More ale, boy."

Father and I locked eyes while he poured. Father nodded, ever so slightly, to let me know that we should listen carefully.

I put the tankard down and stepped back into the shadows.

"They pretend to cry for their countrymen, but what this rabble really wants is an excuse to riot in the streets," Stockdale said, wiping his mouth. "Let's give them what they want—a reason to riot. An insult to their beloved Sons of Liberty."

"Your meaning, sir?" Lieutenant Johnson asked.

"We will arrest Warren and his friends in the upheaval, claiming that Warren's words were the cause."

I may have moved, or gasped, because suddenly Captain Smythe's eyes were on me. Would he bid me leave the room? Would they wait to make their plan above stairs, in the colonel's quarters? I willed my face to look bored. The captain looked away.

"What manner of insult?" he asked the colonel.

I breathed freely again.

"Anything will do. A rock through a window. A well-timed slur. An egg in the face." Stockdale sat up straighter. "Call Ensign Keaton."

I filled more tankards while Ensign Keaton was given his orders. The minute the speech became treasonous, Keaton was to throw an egg at Dr. Warren. Stockdale and his officers would make their arrests in the uproar that was sure to follow.

Colonel Stockdale had raised his glass and recited a poem while the other officers laughed.

> *As for their King John Hancock,*
> *And Adams, if they are taken,*
> *Their heads for signs shall hang on high*
> *Upon that hill called Beacon.*

Father and I had devised a plan of our own, whispering in the kitchen while Mother tended the bar. I was to trip the ensign on his way to the meetinghouse, thus breaking his egg. An overexcited boy racing to get a good seat would hardly be noticed for running into a soldier. Father would have been recognized, so Master Richardson was called on to be my companion instead. I had gone to school early this morning to engage him, and he readily agreed.

"The tyrants!" he said. "They will not rest until they have beaten us into submission. But they have little knowledge of Massachusetts men if they think such a thing is possible. Parliament will submit long before we do."

My schoolmaster was long a friend of the Sons of Liberty and had frequently carried our information to Dr. Warren and Samuel Adams. Today he walked beside me, and I was glad to have his company.

Just then I spotted the ensign. My heart rattled like a drum at full parade march as we increased our speed and came closer and closer to him. I heard sounds around me—Josiah Henshaw proclaiming something to his cronies, black boots pounding, bells ringing—but my eyes saw only the ensign. One hand carefully cupped an egg to his scarlet coat.

Now was the time to trip and fall into him. I leaned forward, but my feet would not leave the cobblestones.

In another second the ensign would be past me and it would be too late. Still, my feet would not do my bidding.

A strong push from behind slammed me into the soldier. I managed to stay upright, but he hit the street with a thud. He rolled over onto his back, clutching his knee, his face distorted with pain. Egg dripped from his hand, staining his white breeches.

Master Richardson stood behind me, breathing hard. "Hurry along, boys," he said, turning to the group behind us and acting as if nothing unusual had occurred. He put a hand on my shoulder and propelled me forward.

I glanced behind me. Two Redcoats came to the aid of the ensign, who had commenced to groan. He appeared unable to stand. Josiah Henshaw's eyes flicked from the schoolmaster to me and back again with a peculiar mixture of curiosity, disdain, and triumph.

My own face burned with shame. If not for Master Richardson, my father's plan would surely have failed.

CHAPTER TWO

Freedom Is the Prize

Old South was full to swarming. All of Boston seemed to be in attendance. A wave of scarlet filled the front pews, and some British officers even sat on the steps leading to the pulpit. Colonel Stockdale was in the first pew, on the aisle. Would he find another way to start a riot and arrest our town leaders in the confusion?

Samuel Adams, in a coat nearly as threadbare as Master Richardson's, greeted the British with all politeness. He must have known the officers were ready to arrest him as soon as they got the signal—the signal Master Richardson had so bravely destroyed when I could not.

Dr. Benjamin Church and other town leaders occupied the deacons' seats, along with John Hancock, who had silk and ruffles enough to satisfy even Josiah Henshaw.

I did not look for my father. Master Richardson sat next to me and nodded more than once. No doubt he was letting our friends know that we had—*he* had—succeeded in our mission.

By the time Dr. Warren arrived, the meetinghouse was so packed that it took him a good while to reach the pulpit. Like the Roman orators of old, he wore a toga over his clothing.

"I mourn over my bleeding country," he said, soon after he began speaking. "With them I weep at her distress, and with them deeply resent the many injuries she has received from the hands of cruel and unreasonable men."

He spoke with dignity, and his language was careful to avoid treason. It warmed my heart to hear him speak of the greatness of our town and of our cause. Many nodded, including Father.

The British stirred but did not rise.

Dr. Warren continued as if they were not there. He spoke of the men who had settled our country, who "bravely threw themselves upon the bosom of the ocean, determined to find a place in which they might enjoy their freedom."

But then our freedom was taken from us, in the form of unfair taxes. We were required to import goods from England, and then taxed for the privilege. It was unjust. Father said so and I agreed. The British were forced to repeal most of their taxes after our protests. Their tea tax remained, and the Sons of Liberty would not stand for it.

Now, as Dr. Warren said, "Our streets are again filled with armed men; our harbor is crowded with ships of war; but these cannot intimidate us."

He was right, and that made me proud. Boston stood firm. A British captain on the pulpit stairs held up a handful of bullets—a warning that muskets were deadlier than words. Dr. Warren dropped a white handkerchief over the captain's hand and continued his address.

"Our liberty must be preserved; it is far dearer than life; we must defend it from the attacks of friends as well as enemies; we cannot suffer even Britons to steal it from us."

Samuel Adams nodded vigorously. Some said his ideas were so radical that they would lead to complete independence from England, but I could not imagine such a thing. Surely the king would come to his senses. Father believed he would, that our rights as free Englishmen would be restored.

"Massachusetts cannot stand for a government

that rules with an iron fist and gives its citizens no freedom, no voice," Father often said. "But the king isn't a tyrant. He will restore our rights when he hears our case."

Others believed that we would be forced to go to war to win back our liberty and break from England completely.

It was as if Dr. Warren heard my thoughts. "An independence from Great Britain is not our aim. No, our wish is that Britain and the colonies, may, like the oak and the ivy, grow and increase in strength together."

I breathed a sigh of relief. I feared what war would bring. Would Father have to fight? Would I? If this morning's test was any measure, I would be a failure as a soldier. I didn't know which scared me more, war or tyranny.

Dr. Warren stood on the side of freedom. War might come, he knew, and he trusted the people of Boston to fight. "However difficult the combat," he said near the end of his speech, "you never will decline it when freedom is the prize."

Colonel Stockdale's forehead creased in a devilish frown. No doubt he was looking for the missing ensign and wondering why the egg had not flown through the air.

When the doctor finished, Samuel Adams took

the pulpit and thanked him for his spirited and elegant oration. He was not one to let the day end without an insult to the Redcoats. He called on the town to make plans for next year's commemoration of the "*bloody massacre.*"

Some of the Redcoats began to hiss. Shouts of "Fie! Fie!" were heard, which were misunderstood and soon became cries of "Fire!" All was panic and confusion. People in the upstairs gallery climbed out of windows and down gutters, sure they were about to be burned alive.

I was thrust this way and that in the frenzied rush for the door. I lost Master Richardson. Josiah pushed past me, his wig askew. Someone knocked into me, and I fell to my knees. Twice I tried to get up, only to be struck down again by the rush of bodies. I buried my head in my hands and screamed, sure that I would be trampled to death. Suddenly there were hands on my shoulders and someone pulled me to my feet.

"There you go, lad," the man said, patting my shoulder with a chuckle.

I grabbed the edge of a pew and fought to catch my breath. The crowd had thinned. Father stood near the doors, anxiously scanning the room.

"Good work, son," he said as I passed by him in the flow of people rushing for the street. "Hurry home now."

On my walk, I turned Dr. Warren's words over and over in my mind.

However difficult the combat, you never will decline it when freedom is the prize.

His sentiment stirred me, but I knew I did not deserve my father's praise. He believed I was the one who stopped the ensign. He thought I had been calm in the panic. I wanted Massachusetts to have her freedoms back, like my father. But I had declined the combat. I had been a coward. Would I ever be worthy of the prize?

CHAPTER THREE

"Tar him! Tar him!"

After the anniversary of the massacre, tense quiet settled over Boston. Many of the Sons of Liberty slipped away to the safety of the countryside. I never told Father of my cowardice, nor did I speak of it with the schoolmaster. I avoided Josiah Henshaw, concentrated on my schoolwork, and helped out more than usual in the tavern.

If the town paid for the tea the Sons of Liberty had destroyed, would King George call his soldiers home? I asked as much at the noon meal one day. Master Richardson joined us, as he often used to before the officers moved in. Mother tended the taproom so Father could eat with us in the kitchen.

"The king and parliament are determined to steal the fruit of our labors without our consent," Father said. "Every effort was made to settle the business with the tea in a peaceful manner."

"Those ships could have sailed back to England with their cargo. That's what happened in every other colony when the people refused to pay the tax," Master Richardson reminded me. "The king's puppet governor here in Boston refused. They aimed to teach us a lesson. To force us to pay. We could not allow it—tyranny must be opposed."

"But things have only gotten worse," I said. "More soldiers. More laws to punish us. If we pay for the tea, would they not go away? Give us our due rights?"

"If we pay for the tea, we will have consented to an unjust tax," Master Richardson said. "We might as well lay down and invite them to pick our pockets."

"Every man has a right to govern himself. A right to enjoy what is acquired by his own labor. A right to freedom," Father told me. "We only demand the same rights as any other free British citizen."

"Without those rights, we become mere slaves to a tyrant," my schoolmaster said. "We cannot allow parliament to intimidate us now."

Their voices had risen in their passion for the subject. Then we heard the front door open and the stomping of officer's boots. The conversation quickly ended. We could not be overheard.

I feared what would happen if peaceful means to bring the conflict to a close came to an end.

One night, as I worked in the tavern, I saw that war would surely come. It was a chill evening, but there was a promise of spring in the air. Rachel, our serving girl, and I ran back and forth from the kitchen to the taproom with plates of food for the officers. The Connecticut colony had driven one thousand sheep overland to Boston for our relief. A saddle of mutton turned on the hearth; Mother had roasted potatoes and made corn bread. It was a real feast.

Father quietly surveyed the room while he drew ale and poured rum. Mother busied herself over the cook pot. My little sister, Sarah, who was but three, supped in the kitchen. There was a low rumble of voices, the occasional call for drink, but all was peaceful.

Then the door slammed open and a group of regular soldiers rushed in, dragging a man between them. They stopped in front of Lieutenant Colonel Stockdale.

"Private Osborne, colonel," said the regular who seemed to be in charge.

Colonel Stockdale was none too pleased to have

his evening meal disturbed. He sat back and sucked a piece of mutton from between his teeth. "Yes, private?"

"This peddler has been promising to help us desert the king's service, in exchange for our muskets."

"I didn't. I didn't," the man stammered. His eyes were fixed on the colonel's boots.

"My soldiers say you did," Stockdale said. "What proof have you that you didn't?"

"I . . . I have no proof," the peddler said. He jutted out his chin in a determined manner. "Nor do they have proof that I did."

The officers gathered around Stockdale. "Prove it. Prove it," they chanted, drowning out the man's words. They seemed more interested in revenge than in the truth. General Gage, the military governor of Massachusetts, had threatened to execute all deserters from the British army and any who helped them. More than one soldier was shot on the Common, caught in the act of trying to leave Boston. Still, everyone knew that Redcoats continued to creep out of the town in search of a new life, leaving their uniforms behind. Some were even training our Minutemen in the ways of war.

Father's hands were underneath the bar, no doubt reaching for the musket that was hidden there. I froze. If he pulled it out in defense of the man, surely the British would kill them both. Mother rushed in and put her hand on his arm. The kitchen door was ajar and I saw that Sarah watched, her little face pale and frightened. I stepped in front of the door so she would not see, but my sudden movement put one of the soldiers on alert. He swung around and pointed his musket at me. His bayonet was fixed, candlelight flickering against the shiny blade. My breathing stopped. I tried to stand still, but my body shook. I thought I might fall right into the blade.

Mother stepped forward and pushed the weapon upright. "There's no call for that," she said evenly.

Would he turn his bayonet on Mother? I wanted to step between them, but once again, my feet would not do my bidding.

Mother held the soldier's gaze steady. "There's no call for any of this," she said in a lighter tone, urging the men back to their seats. "Come, finish this nice meal I've made for you. A free glass of rum for all."

But the officers didn't want to be distracted. I could see it on their faces. They were hungry for another opportunity to teach the people of Boston a lesson.

"Surely this has been a misunderstanding," Father said.

Colonel Stockdale waved his saber over his head to call for quiet. There was immediate silence. We waited to hear his verdict.

He leaned back and surveyed the peddler. "Let's give these Boston rebels the same punishment they heap on their own enemies," he said. "Give the man a new coat. Make it out of tar and decorate it with feathers."

The man gasped, but the colonel simply continued his instructions. "Carry him through the streets so all can see what happens to those who defy the king."

"Tar him! Tar him!" the officers chanted.

I cringed. The Sons of Liberty had indeed tarred and feathered some of their enemies. It was a terrible thing, and now the Redcoats were using this poor man to get their revenge.

The soldiers rushed to their task like boys to a game of ringer, only it was a life they played with, not marbles. Some men did not survive such torture.

I watched from the window as they dragged the peddler onto Fish Street. Our tavern sign, a blue whale, creaked in the wind. The soldiers laughed and sang "Yankee Doodle," a song that mocked us, as they dragged the man toward the wharves.

The peddler's eyes darted around wildly in search of help. For a moment they landed on me. I stepped back into the shadows.

CHAPTER FOUR

Shots Fired in Lexington

April, 1775

Colonel Stockdale spent more and more time at the Province House with General Gage. When at the tavern he was often shut in his room with his officers. Each morning at school Master Richardson greeted me with raised eyebrows, but I could only shake my head. I had no secret news to report.

Rachel generally cleaned the officer's rooms, but one day Mother took over the task and saw that Colonel Stockdale had maps on his desk.

The next morning I nodded in answer to my assistant schoolmaster's silent question. During our morning writing assignment, I asked to go to the necessary out back. Master Richardson met me outside the door upon my return.

"What news, Daniel?" he asked.

"Stockdale studies maps. The route to Concord is marked," I told him.

He nodded. "Guns and gunpowder both are being stored in Concord. They must mean to capture it and end any chance of rebellion before it begins."

"Are any of the Sons of Liberty in hiding there?" I asked. I knew that some had slipped quietly out of Boston.

"John Hancock and Samuel Adams are staying in Lexington," Master Richardson said. "Was there anything more?

"No," I told him. "Nothing more."

"Good work, Daniel. I'll tell Dr. Warren this evening. Keep your ears open." Then he raised his voice as he opened the door to our schoolroom and ushered me in. "Stop wasting time, Daniel Prescott. There's work to be done."

I took my seat and raised my quill.

In the middle of April the grenadiers, the biggest and best soldiers in the king's army, along with the light infantry, were relieved of their regular duty. We heard they were to learn new exercises, but no one believed that story. Each day brought new activity and new rumors.

"They're planning something," Father said to me the next evening.

"Do you think they mean to seize the gunpowder?" I asked him.

"Aye." Father nodded. "And mayhap Samuel Adams, too. We must be on alert for any crumb of information."

I was as still as possible when I waited on the officers, willing them to forget I was there. But I learned nothing new that would help our cause.

A few days later I watched while longboats, used for rowing soldiers across the waters that surrounded Boston, were launched from the men-of-war ships in the harbor. A thin strip of salt marsh—the Boston Neck—was all that connected the town to the rest of the colony. Father had thought the longboats might be a trick to fool us into thinking the soldiers would travel by water to Cambridge and then march to Lexington and Concord when they really planned to reach Cambridge by marching over the Neck. Dr. Warren had men at the ready to warn the people in the countryside whether the Redcoats set out from Boston by land or by sea. Our militia would be ready to defend our gunpowder and protect Samuel Adams from being seized by the British.

That night the air was thick with the sounds of rattling drums, clanking muskets, and stomping boots. Officers barked orders. Soldiers obeyed. I longed for information. So did Father. Colonel Stockdale was out, but the tavern was crowded with soldiers who were not part of the night's plan. Father and Mother were too busy to leave the tavern. Father bid me to try and find out what was happening.

I slipped out the kitchen door and ran to the Common. Along with a hundred others I watched in the bright, cold moonlight as Redcoats filled the longboats and were ferried to Cambridge. Colonel Stockdale was at their head.

Josiah Henshaw stood about looking important while his father was in discussion with an officer. I greeted him, but my aim was to see what I could overhear.

"The Redcoats will soon put an end to this silly rebellion," Josiah boasted. "And we can begin importing goods again."

I shrugged, hoping he would be quiet long enough for me to hear what his father said. He was not. He prattled on and on about the fine things he would have when trading ships once more filled the harbor, and the delicious food that would grace his table.

"I am to have all the lemons and pimientos and sugar I want. Cakes—lots and lots of cakes."

I only grunted in response and thought of the British and their muskets in our tavern. How dare he speak of cakes while soldiers threatened our very lives? I wanted to shove him. But to do so would only gain his father's attention. I willed Josiah to be quiet so I could hear. But his father's conversation was long over before Josiah had run out of imaginary treats to boast of.

Master Richardson had a better opportunity. After catching my eye and nodding briefly, he strolled up and entered a quiet conversation with Mr. Henshaw. No doubt he was trying to learn something of use to the Patriots. I ran home and shared what I had seen.

The next morning I went to school as usual, but Boston was crazy with guessing games. How desperate we were for news! More Redcoats left our town that morning, marching over the Neck. Finally, around ten o'clock, we heard riders galloping through the streets with reports.

Two hundred boys could not attend their hand-writing on such a morning. We buzzed like bees at their honey. Our schoolmaster had not yet appeared. His assistant, Master Richardson, tried to maintain order, but it was impossible.

"Daniel Prescott," he said sternly, "go and gather whatever information you can. Perhaps when we know what has happened you boys will settle down to your schoolwork."

"Why him?" Josiah Henshaw asked.

Others shouted, "I want to go! I want to go!"

Master Richardson dropped the quill he was mending and pounded on his desk. "Silence! Daniel Prescott is to go. The rest of you will continue your lesson."

I raced out of the classroom and ran down Middle Street toward Faneuil Hall, stopping to listen whenever I spied a messenger.

A group of townspeople surrounded a man on horseback. He had been riding hard. "They've done it," he said. "The Redcoats have fired on the people."

I hoped his information was false, but too many confirmed it. Shots had been fired in Lexington.

"Are you certain?" I asked.

The messenger nodded. "I've seen the dead with my own eyes." Then he rode off.

I shuddered. Blood had been shed. My mind raced. What did this mean for Boston? For Father?

I ran to the Common. One man said the British had seized all and won the day.

"Why would Gage send more soldiers this morning if that were true?" I asked.

"The Massachusetts militia has driven them back!" shouted another rider. "The Redcoats are retreating!"

One man claimed that the Redcoats had shot women and children, another that they had scampered away like frightened rats when faced with Massachusetts's might. I pieced together what facts I could and trudged back to school. I had no more energy for running.

My chest heaved as I tried to speak the words. "Shots were fired in Lexington. Many are dead. I think the Redcoats are being driven back to Boston by our militia." My voice wavered. My heart was divided. I felt pride in the farmers, hunters, blacksmiths, storekeepers, and fishermen who had stood up against the mightiest army on earth. They had said no to tyranny. At the same time, I feared war. I especially feared the British revenge that would surely follow. They shot at unarmed citizens in the Boston Massacre. They tarred and feathered the peddler for mere suspicion. How many would they kill now?

"Have the British really begun it?" Master Richardson asked.

"They've begun it and they'll end it," Josiah Henshaw said, jumping to his feet. His words were all bluster, but there was fear in his eyes.

Timothy Otis drowned him out. "Liberty!" he

shouted. Soon all the boys who sided with the Patriots joined the chant. "Liberty! Liberty! Liberty!"

I held my silence, as always. But I saw that Josiah's eyes flicked from me to the assistant schoolmaster and back again.

"Go home, boys," Master Richardson said. "Go home."

Citizens stood about the town in small clumps, sharing gossip. Redcoats snarled. The people snarled back.

A man walked up to a soldier and shook a fist in his face. "You'll get your due now," he threatened. "You'll get your due."

The soldier only mocked him, but there was a nervous edge to his laughter.

That afternoon we learned that there was fighting in Concord, too, and the Redcoats were on the run. They were returning to Boston. I ran for the top of Beacon Hill, which afforded a view of Charlestown.

Just before sunset there was firing in the distance. Charlestown appeared deserted. People must have been hiding in their homes, or perhaps they had already left the town.

It was nearly dark when I saw long columns of Redcoats marching into Charlestown. Behind them, the sun sank into the hills of Lexington in a fiery red ball. The flash of musket fire twinkled like stars in the gathering darkness. The shots seemed to come out of nowhere, and I thought militiamen must have been hiding behind trees, walls, and houses.

A cold rain began to fall as the wounded Redcoats were loaded into the longboats and ferried across the Charles River to Boston. I had to run back to the tavern to help Mother and Father, but not before I saw men in bandages limp off the boats. I recalled how strong and sure they seemed just yesterday. How different they looked tonight, broken and bloody.

All manner of carts and carriages lumbered to the ferry house to carry those wounded who could not walk. Wooden wheels creaked and rattled against the cobblestones. Horses whinnied. People spoke in whispers.

Father was out when I got back to the tavern. Mother tended bar, her face creased with worry. Colonel Stockdale arrived a couple of hours later. His face and his scarlet coat were covered in dirt and sweat. There was a bandage on his thigh and bloodstains on his white breeches. I wondered how many Massachusetts men he had shot, and my fingers burned to throw a tankard at him.

He strode up to the bar.

"Rum, madam," he said to my mother.

The officers gathered around him, waiting.

He raised his glass high. "I curse the Englishman who first set foot on this savage land," he said bitterly.

Soon the officers were all shouting about how they would pay the people back. The violent acts they described grew more and more deadly with each drink they took. They cheered one another with cries of "Huzzah! Huzzah!"

Father had returned. His jaw was set, his teeth clenched. Like me, he could do nothing in the face of their boasting.

The Redcoats claimed that the men of Lexington had fired the first shots.

"Not true," Father muttered when we were alone. "The British opened fire. The militia only defended themselves and their property."

We wondered what would happen next. One thing seemed sure: we were at war.

★ CHAPTER FIVE ★

Under Siege

May, 1775

After the battles at Lexington and Concord, it was rumored that militia companies were pouring into the country around Boston. Many of them could be seen from the hills and rooftops of Boston. Within a week we heard that some fifteen thousand men from Massachusetts, New Hampshire, Connecticut, and Rhode Island had formed a new army—the New England army. They trapped the British inside the town, and us along with them. We were under siege.

General Gage strengthened his fortifications on the Neck. We were cut off from any contact with the country.

The next days were a tangle of disorder. Dread

reigned in Boston. The Patriots feared that Gage would destroy us from within. The Loyalists feared the New England army would destroy us from without. Everyone feared starvation. With both the harbor and the Neck closed, where would our necessaries of life come from?

"What will we do for food? How will we fill our bellies?" Mother asked.

"British supply ships will continue to arrive for as long as the Redcoats are in Boston," Father told us. "The officers will make sure they are well fed even if the regular soldiers are not. Unless they leave the tavern, we will have food and fuel enough to cook for them and for ourselves."

"What about everyone else?" I asked. I thought of Timothy Otis and my other friends at school. Could I eat British food while they starved?

Father grimaced. "I hope Gage has sense enough to let people leave the town."

"Should we leave, too, if that is the case?" Mother asked.

I had never thought of leaving Boston. I knew no other place.

Father shook his head. "There's no telling what would happen to the tavern if we left. And how will we earn a living elsewhere?"

And so we stayed. I did not yet know whether to

be happy or sad about that. I feared what the coming months would bring.

General Gage ordered the citizens to surrender their firearms. Father went to Faneuil Hall and handed over a broken musket, but he kept his other one. It was no longer under the bar, but now hidden underneath a loose floorboard in my room above the kitchen.

On the Sabbath following the battle, Gage met with the town selectmen and agreed to allow the Patriots to leave the town—as long as they left their weapons and food behind. Once again long lines formed at Faneuil Hall, where people pleaded with and bribed the officers for passes.

That night Colonel Stockdale had six hams, a basket of eggs, a barrel of flour, and three cackling chickens delivered to the tavern. The chickens were given to Sarah to care for, and she promptly named them Robin Goodfellow, Jacky Juggle, and Billy Bilk, after the characters in a fairy tale I sometimes read to her. I feared what would happen if Colonel Stockdale insisted on chicken for dinner, but at least eggs would be plentiful until then.

The fleeing Patriots made a strange parade. Sarah and I watched carriages and carts, filled to overflowing, slowly make their way toward the Neck. At first Sarah clapped and waved, enjoying the show. Soon even her bright spirit was darkened by the mood. I gripped her hand too tightly and she pulled it away with a whimper.

Soldiers rammed their bayonets into featherbeds, searching for hidden food and weapons. A cart was toppled in the search. I wished I could ram a bayonet into the soldiers, overturn them as if they were nothing. Instead I helped the tired-looking woman rescue her household goods from the mud. Then I spotted a schoolmate in the crowd.

"Timothy!" I yelled.

"We're bound for Salem," he shouted. "I'll see you when the Sons of Liberty have won the war!"

I waved good-bye, but could say nothing. I admired his bravery. It would be grand to be able to say such a thing in front of so many Redcoats. My work in the tavern prevented me. I had also seen British anger up close, and I did not have the daring to provoke it.

By the end of the week, there appeared to be two or three soldiers in the town for every citizen. The streets were strangely empty. Many people had left their doors open in their rush to leave. Some Redcoats and even a few Boston boys freely wandered in and took what they wanted. My days were strange, too. School had been closed as soon as the war began. I busied myself at the tavern. There was work enough to do.

The British built up fortifications within the town, while we heard rumors that the Patriots did the same on the outside. The New England army set up headquarters in Cambridge.

The Redcoats drilled all day. By night the officers gambled at cards and dice and made fun of the Patriot troops that surrounded them. In early May I overheard Colonel Stockdale say that four more regiments of soldiers were expected from Halifax any day.

"Gage will have to stop crying about his lack of soldiers, and drive this rabble from the countryside," Colonel Stockdale growled.

I feared for the New England army. Could their bravery and love of liberty stand up to a large force of Redcoats?

Father had the same question.

That night I woke to discover him in my room. His candle made great monstrous shadows on the wall as he quietly lifted the floorboard and removed his musket. I followed him down the ladder into the kitchen.

"What—" I started to ask, but he signaled me to be silent.

The fire was banked for the night. Surely it was not time to start breakfast. Had Father decided to go hunting? Mother was at the table, filling a haversack.

Her mouth was set in a grim line, the way it was when I got caught playing marbles on the Sabbath. I noted the items in front of her: mug, canteen, knife, fork, spoon, plate, cartridge box.

I slumped at the table, resting my head on one hand. Great yawns overtook my body and I shivered.

"Three o'clock," I heard the town watchman announce from Fish Street. The familiar phrase "and all is well," did not follow. It had not followed since the war began.

I struggled to blink away the fog of sleep.

Father checked the taproom to make sure it was empty and then laid a hand on my shoulder. "Daniel, I am going to join the army," he said. "Another battle is expected any day. When England sees how serious we are, parliament will restore our rights. I aim to do my part before it's all over."

Suddenly I was wide awake. What if Father was killed in this battle? He could even be shot for leaving town without a pass.

Father did not take his eyes from me. Gradually I guessed the meaning in them. He wanted me to go with him. The idea filled me with dread. I didn't want to leave Mother and Sarah. I did not want to fight in a battle. I was afraid, but how could I disappoint him?

"I'll get my things," I mumbled.

Mother gasped, but said nothing. The determined jut of her chin and the way she eyeballed Father reminded me of one of Josiah Henshaw's staring contests.

"No," he said to me gently. "I need you to stay here—to help your mother and sister. And Colonel Stockdale still has valuable information that must be passed along."

But who would protect us from the Redcoats if Father were not here? How could I possibly keep spying on the colonel without Father to help me, to tell me what to do?

"But how—" I sputtered. "How can you leave? How can we stay here once they find out?"

"Colonel Stockdale arranged for a pass," Father said, showing me a piece of paper. "I told him that my dear mother in Connecticut is dying, and I have to go to her. If I leave now I can reach the encampment by first light."

Father's mother had died before I was born, that I knew. He had been raised up in Connecticut. The son of a whaler, he had become one himself. But Mother wanted a man with two feet on solid ground, as she said, and Father gave up whaling when he married her. That's why Prescott Tavern's sign was a blue whale.

Some of the Sons of Liberty took their business

elsewhere when the Redcoats moved in, but we did not suffer the same insults as others. I think many of them suspected our secret work.

"The New England army needs your sharp eyes and fast feet here in Boston," Father said.

I didn't see how I could continue our work without him. It was the work of a man, not a boy.

He seemed to read my mind. "You have been very brave," he said. "Master Richardson remains in town, along with a few other Patriots. Depend on him. He'll be sure to pass any valuable information along to the new army."

My mind flashed back to March the sixth. Father still believed I had acted bravely. If I told him my shameful secret now, would he change his plans? Part of me wanted to, but another part valued his praise too much. "I would rather be fighting at your side," I lied, staring at the candle.

"No, Daniel," he said. "Your duty is here. Honor your mother, and make me proud."

I nodded, not trusting myself to speak, as he pulled me into a hug.

In the bedroom off the kitchen he cradled Sarah in his arms for a moment before moving her from her own small bed into the one he shared with Mother. She whimpered and then rolled over, fast asleep again.

He hugged Mother for a good long time before shouldering his haversack and picking up his musket. He turned to look at each of us one more time before closing the door behind him. In the breeze, the candle flickered and went out.

CHAPTER SIX

The Whale
Swims South

I didn't know if post could come to us from the Patriot camp, but every day I hoped for a letter from Father. I wanted to know if he had arrived safely, how he spent his days. Did he sleep in a tent? What did he eat? Did he have musket balls enough?

Two days after he left for the New England army, new British soldiers arrived from Halifax. I worried that the British would mount an attack before Father was ready to defend himself. But no attack was forthcoming. Then I overheard the officers gossiping and, mayhap, I discovered the reason.

Since the schools had been closed, I no longer saw Master Richardson every day, but we had worked out a signal when I had news for the Patriots. A blacksmith had copied the blue whale from our tavern sign and forged it into a boot scraper we kept outside the front door. It was good and heavy. No one would think to move it—except me.

I turned the whale north, toward Canada, when I had no news. When I turned the scraper around so the whale was swimming south to the West Indies, I had British secrets to share. That afternoon I turned it around, and early the next morning I went to meet my schoolmaster.

After building up the kitchen fire, I grabbed our water buckets and headed for the meeting place: the town pump in North Square. Master Richardson's rooms were in a house nearby. Unfortunately, others in the house could not be trusted, and so we met in public.

I took my time, enjoying the early morning. The spring sunshine was warm on my face. I took a deep breath of Boston air—salty, fishy, Boston air. There were no Redcoats about at the moment, and I could almost pretend that the town was not under siege. But the pump was near deserted, reminding me of how many citizens had left. I missed the chatter and the gossip of those who used to gather here. The few people who waited for a turn looked pinched and sour.

Soon Master Richardson stood beside me.

"Good day, Daniel," he said, loudly for all around us to hear. "How are things at Prescott's Tavern?"

"Very well," I answered, just as loudly.

Our conversation was of no importance until I bent over the pump.

"What news, Daniel?" he asked.

I lowered my voice. "Three new generals sailed from London on the *Cerberus*," I told him. "One by the name of Howe. Stockdale expects Gage to attack the Patriots as soon as they land and he has their advice."

Master Richardson only nodded. I knew he passed on everything I told him, but to whom remained a mystery. It was best I did not know. I trusted that the knowledge would eventually reach General Ward's headquarters in Cambridge. I wondered what Father was doing, and if he was ready for a battle.

"Have you news for me? News of my father?" I asked.

"He is well," Master Richardson said. "I have a letter for you." He patted his jacket to show me where it was.

I wanted to rip it from him and read it immediately, I was so excited to have news of Father. But I forced myself to wait until he could slip it to me without anyone noticing. I filled the second bucket and pulled the yoke over my shoulders.

I wished the Patriots could charge into Boston and drive the British into the sea! The Neck was well guarded by the Redcoats, however, and eight British warships sat in the harbor, ready to fire their cannons. The Patriots could not stand up to such might.

Master Richardson raised his voice again, drawing me away from my thoughts. "I trust that you continue to practice your hand, now that the schools are closed."

"Aye, sir, when I can," I said.

"Perhaps I will come see you one day soon."

"I would like that, sir."

As we moved away from the pump, he lowered his voice again, unraveling the threads on the cuff of his frayed coat. "Do you need help at the tavern now that your father has gone? With food so dear . . ." His voice trailed off in embarrassment.

The cost of food had doubled, tripled, and then doubled again. Many were hungry. It pained me to tell Master Richardson that we now employed a Redcoat to man the tap in his off-duty hours. Mother and I had discussed hiring the schoolmaster. We knew his purse was already nearly empty, and now his school salary was stopped. But we worried that British tongues would stop wagging freely with the addition of a new barman who wasn't one of their own.

Master Richardson's face turned from hopeful to bitter. He said nothing.

"Can the army pay you wages?" I asked.

"My work is secret. And General Ward has no funds," Master Richardson said, shaking his head. "He hopes the Continental Congress in Philadelphia will bring all thirteen colonies to the cause and take charge of the army, but I am not hopeful. I risk my life daily for their cause, but I think the Sons of Liberty would let me starve."

"But the cause is just, is it not? Liberty. Freedom from tyranny," I said. "I've heard you speak of it many times."

"Liberty." He snorted. "What good is liberty if we all die of starvation?"

We took leave of each other. I tarried to watch the schoolmaster walk toward his rooms, troubled by his words—so troubled that I barely noticed Josiah Henshaw running after him. I ducked out of sight. Josiah Henshaw was the very last person I wished to see when I carried buckets like a servant. It was only later that I wondered what had drawn him from Beacon Hill so early in the morning.

CHAPTER SEVEN

A Spy Mission

Two days after the new generals arrived, we woke at dawn to distant roars and booms of cannon fire. Sarah whimpered in Mother's arms while we tried to discover the reason. One of General Stockdale's men informed us that the Patriots and the Redcoats fought over the livestock and the hay on Hog's and Noddle's islands in the harbor. We soon became used to cannonading from both sides.

British General "Gentleman Johnny" Burgoyne had promised to make elbow room in Boston when he learned that mere colonists held the Redcoats in Boston, but Gage still made no move on the Patriot camp outside of town. I waited and wondered.

One afternoon, Stockdale was called to a meeting with General Gage, and then again the next. He and the other officers were clipped and terse in the tavern. They were planning something, that I knew, but what? Mother spotted maps on the colonel's desk while changing his bed linens, but he came in upon her and rolled them up before she learned their subject.

I thought I must search Stockdale's rooms when no one was about.

"Don't do anything foolish, Daniel," Mother warned me. "No one expects you to risk your life. One Prescott in the line of fire is enough. You be safe."

Despite her warnings, I thought I must try. Father would not come home until the war was over. What if I could hurry the end of the conflict? I might be a coward when it came to fighting on a battlefield, but the tavern was my home. This was something I could do.

Stockdale was once again called to Gage's headquarters. The other officers were parading the soldiers on the Common. I took advantage of the empty tavern to search the colonel's rooms and slipped upstairs without telling Mother of my plans.

I unrolled the parchment on his desk. It was a map of the town of Boston and the lands surrounding the town. To the north was Charlestown peninsula. To the south, Dorchester. Each of these peninsulas had large hills overlooking Boston Harbor and the town. The Patriot army was camped between them, but neither army controlled the hills.

Even I could see that command of those hills would mean command of the surrounding country, including Boston. The whole town could be swept away by the British big guns. From the markings on Stockdale's map, I guessed that the Redcoats planned to fortify the hills of Charlestown or Dorchester, or both. From there, they could easily scatter the New England army into the countryside, away from Boston, and break the siege.

I was studying the map when I heard the colonel's voice, commanding some of his officers to join him upstairs. The rooms had been cleaned that morning. I had no reason to be above stairs.

I slipped into the hall. There was no escape. No way to get downstairs without being seen. The door to a room shared by three of the officers was ajar. I dashed behind it and pushed it closed.

Footsteps approached—their pounding on the stairs as loud as cannon fire. I recognized the high, nervous voice of Captain Smythe and the deep rumble of Lieutenant Johnson—two of the men who had taken such pleasure in the tarring and feathering of the peddler some weeks ago. I cringed behind the door and prayed they would not need to enter their own chamber, but only the colonel's.

One set of footsteps slowed and seemed to hesitate. I imagined a hand on the doorknob and braced myself for the blow that would surely follow my discovery. But the boots continued across the hall. My breath came out in a long sigh when I heard Stockdale slam his own door behind them.

With shaking knees, I crept into the hall. Stockdale's roar could be heard through the closed door.

"Howe and Burgoyne have finally convinced Grandma to act," Stockdale said. "Grandma" was what Stockdale called General Gage when he thought no one but his trusted officers were about. "We'll break this rebellion once and for all."

I couldn't make out what the other officers said. Someone shuffled papers.

"We're to take this hill," Stockdale said.

Which hill? There was more talk from the other officers. Then another piece of valuable intelligence came though the door in Stockdale's booming voice.

"June eighteenth."

I calculated the days. That was ten days hence. Time enough to get word to Master Richardson. Time enough to warn Father and the rest of the Patriots. Time enough for them to be ready. But which hill?

There was movement in the room. I ran down the

stairs as if on cat's feet and laid my signal—turning the boot scraper so that the whale swam toward the West Indies. That night in the taproom I kept my mouth shut and my ears open. I poured the rum a little too freely and soon I was rewarded. Dorchester was on the lips of more than one officer. I believed I knew their full plan.

The next morning, I went to North Square. Master Richardson was not there. Nor was he in his rooms. Had he missed the signal? I went in search of him.

Something drew me to Beacon Hill. I thought I might get a look at the Patriot camp. I wanted to be able to picture Father. To have some notion of what his life was like there. The last time I had been on this hill, I watched wounded Redcoats limp off longboats on their way back from Charlestown.

Today the harbor was quiet, and it was the fancy homes that held my attention. Many of them were deserted, but not the Henshaw home.

I had a notion to watch the house. I slipped into the alley and waited. It wasn't long before my patience was repaid. Master Richardson appeared with Mr. Henshaw and Josiah.

I followed them. The distance was too great to make out their conversation, but all three looked mighty friendly. I pitied my schoolmaster for having to be pleasant with such as them. How often would he have to bite his tongue to avoid lashing out at their Loyalist remarks? I hoped the information that came his way would be truly valuable.

He took his leave of Mr. Henshaw and Josiah at the bottom of the hill, shaking hands all around. I had meant to speak to the schoolmaster, but hesitated. I couldn't say why I did not approach Master Richardson then. I hung back as he walked past the tavern. Surely he noticed the boot scraper had been turned.

The next morning, the assistant schoolmaster was at the pump. His wig was newly powdered, and he expressed none of the bitterness of our last meeting. A worry flitted through me like the silver notes of a fife. I wished for Father, for his wise council. Then I reminded myself of the help the schoolmaster had given me on the anniversary of the Boston Massacre, and his many political conversations with Father. Master Richardson was a true friend to the Sons of Liberty.

I told him all.

"Stockdale has maps of Charlestown and Dorchester Heights. The Redcoats will fortify Dorchester Heights on June eighteenth, and mayhap the hills of Charlestown, too."

The schoolmaster looked grave as I repeated the colonel's words. "They plan to break the rebellion once and for all," I told him.

He asked many questions, which I answered as best as I could. Then I asked one of my own.

"Does Josiah Henshaw continue his schooling?"

He drew back, looking around us as if for a set of listening ears. "I tutor young Mr. Henshaw privately," the schoolmaster told me. "It's a splendid opportunity."

I nodded. Mr. Henshaw was a friend to General Gage himself and important intelligence might come the schoolmaster's way while in that house. But worry ran through me again. Master Richardson knew my father was a Patriot, and all of my secrets, too. What if the Henshaws had discovered the master's true employment and laid a trap? What if my family got caught in it?

CHAPTER EIGHT

The Patriot Camp

June, 1775

It was not long before I had cause to turn the whale again. He swam south to warmer seas to let Master Richardson know I wanted to meet. Only this time, instead of passing secrets to the schoolmaster, I asked him to pass secrets on to me. I was to make my own trip to the Patriot camp!

My aunt Abigail, Mother's sister, worried us daily about her two sons. Paul was fifteen and John, seventeen. They had disappeared and she was frantic. Mother and I believed that they had swum over to the Patriot camp one night and joined the army. Aunt Abigail was convinced they had been hurt or captured.

She soon learned that one Boston mother had been given a pass to go to the Patriot camp to search for her son. Unwilling to leave her other children, she pressed Mother to allow me to go. I did not think my cousins would come back to Boston on my urging, but knowing with certainty where they were would bring her some relief. I welcomed the chance to visit Father and see the camp.

Aunt Abigail's pleas were so pitiful that Mother finally consented to the plan. My aunt was just as pitiful with Colonel Stockdale, and he arranged for a pass. I was to carry nothing with me that might aide the rebels, but I could go in search of my cousins.

Master Richardson's concern for my safety outweighed his pleasure at the idea of my trip. He bid me to rethink the whole notion.

"Colonel Stockdale expects it now," I said, filling my first bucket. "And there will be no peace in our house until Aunt Abigail has word of John and Paul. I must go."

He stared into the distance. Worry wrinkled his brow.

I thought to change the subject. "How are things at the Henshaw home?" I asked, bending over the pump.

"They are slow to trust me," he answered. "I haven't been able to uncover any information, although Gage himself supped with the family last night."

I thought mayhap the schoolmaster had other listening ears around Boston in addition to my own, but he had no intelligence for me to take to the Patriot leaders. Instead, he cautioned me again and again not to mention his name in camp.

"I have reason to believe there are British spies about," he told me.

Master Richardson took his leave, and I walked back to the tavern with the yoke over my shoulders, a full bucket of water on either side.

Early Thursday morning, I saddled our horse Star and set off. I hadn't been out of Boston since the fighting began and was surprised by the new fortifications at the Neck. As I approached, three soldiers leveled their muskets at me, ready to shoot.

My hands tightened on the reins. Star threw her head back and snorted, sensing my fear. She skittered sideways on the narrow Neck, trying to get away from the soldiers. I forced my hands to loosen their grip and spoke to her in a soothing tone. She was a good horse and generally a calm one, but the constant cannonading from both sides had left her excitable. If she took fright and ran off at a full gallop, I would surely end up with a musket ball in my back.

I dismounted and held her bridle, walking slowly forward as I crooned. The soldiers kept their guns leveled, although I obviously had no weapon of my own. With shaking hands I stretched out my arm to give the guard nearest me my pass. Star danced in place. Her eyes were wide, her ears pinned back. Suddenly I was afraid, too. Would I meet similar guards at the Patriot camp?

The Redcoats examined my pass and waved me through.

Soon I was on a rise overlooking the encampment. It stretched as far as my eye could see, from Roxbury all the way to Cambridge and beyond. How would I ever find Father in such a place?

Boston Harbor had been closed to all but British ships carrying British soldiers for such a long time that I had forgotten how different ordinary colonial men could be. As I rode along, searching for a familiar face, I found all manner of men and all manner of shelter.

There was nothing like the neat military rows of tents that dotted Boston Common or the unvarying dress of the Redcoats. Here everything was higgledy-piggledy. Shelter had been built from whatever the men could find—logs, boards, sailcloth, stones, and even dirt. Many were about to fall over; others had the appearance of a comfortable home long lived in.

The men themselves were topsy-turvy. Few wore

uniforms, and it seemed that those who did had each designed their own. I spotted sailors with bandannas tied around their heads, straw hats, beaver caps, and many sweat-stained felt hats.

I finally saw a Boston man and asked after Father. The man pointed me toward Cambridge.

I slowly made my way in that direction, carefully avoiding the necessaries and the cook fires, both of which seemed to be established wherever the men happened to be when the need for one, or the hunger for the other, overcame them.

Finally, near midday, I came upon Cambridge. A militia company from New Hampshire offered to share their meal with me—rabbits roasting on a spit. I had not tasted fresh meat in weeks. My mouth watered, but I couldn't wait to find Father. I had not seen him for nearly two months.

They teased me for being a Boston man.

"No doubt he's a firebrand like old Samuel Adams, ready to sever all ties with the king," one man said.

Others scoffed at the idea. "Cut off all ties with England?" they jeered. "We're Englishmen!"

I had heard whispered talk of full independence from England, but I could see that even the Patriot soldiers thought such a move was too drastic. We were Englishmen, fighting for our rights as such.

All the soldiers seemed to know that the Redcoats

were about to make a bold move, and all promised the war would soon be over. They claimed the people of Massachusetts—indeed all the colonies—would enjoy our rights once again.

Father spied me before I saw him. "Daniel!"

His hair had come loose from its queue and flew behind him as he raced toward me. Star recognized him and began to trot. I held tight to the reins. "Mother and Sarah are well," I shouted, guessing at the cause of alarm in his voice. "I have a pass to search for my cousins. Aunt Abigail needs to know where they are if she is to have any peace."

Father patted Star's nose while he caught his breath. His eyes drank me in, and I could see that they were wet. I had often suspected that Father missed the adventure he found at sea. He loved to entertain the tavern's customers with wild tales about his whaling days. But I had always counted myself lucky that he had left the sea behind and stayed home with us. I worried when he joined the militia that the adventure of war would steal him from the family. But now I could see that Father had missed me as much as I missed him.

I embraced him, then pulled back, embarrassed to be acting the boy in front of soldiers.

"You've grown taller," Father said.

I threw my shoulders back. "Mother's altering

a pair of your old breeches for when I outgrow my own," I told him.

"Aye, you'll be as tall as me soon," he said.

Father was deeply tanned by spending so much time outdoors, and he was what Mother would call unkempt. His waistcoat was torn, and he looked as if he hadn't had a bath in all the weeks since he left Boston. His hair was loose about his face, he was badly shaven, and dirt filled every crook and crevice of his person.

He looked down and tried to dust himself off with a laugh. "Mother would have my head, would she not?" he asked.

I nodded. He seemed to enjoy his dirtiness, and my astonishment.

"I was digging an entrenchment," he said. "Knee-deep I was, when I heard that a boy was in camp, asking after me. I threw my shovel into the air and ran. But tell me the news of home."

I gave him all the news of Mother and Sarah, and learned that Master Richardson had twice slipped out of Boston to pass along my intelligence.

"You've done a fine job, Daniel," Father told me, his hand on my shoulder.

I nodded, feeling grown up and strong. "I'm proud to help," I told him. It felt good to do something other than serve British soldiers at the tavern. "What will you do when the Redcoats take Dorchester Heights?" I asked. "Will there be a battle?"

Father shrugged. "That's not for a lowly soldier to know," he said cheerfully. "We await orders and hope for the best."

At the tavern, Father was always in charge and in control. It was hard to believe that he did not know all, but he seemed content with the life of an ordinary soldier. He even stopped to get permission from his captain before taking me to find my cousins. They had joined a company that was camped near Roxbury, and as I suspected, they refused to return to Boston with me.

"Not until King George calls his soldiers home," John said.

Paul, as he always did, agreed with his brother. "I won't desert my company, or my brother," he added. He waved his arm around, indicating the camp. "This will all be over by winter. Tell Mother we'll see her then."

Then they wrote a letter on the back of my pass. I wasn't sure if the Redcoat guards would allow me to bring it to Aunt Abigail, but at least I could tell her that her sons were unharmed.

Father and I agreed that I should spend the night in camp. He was fine company as we made our way back to his tent, entertaining me with stories of his fellow soldiers. Sometimes, despite the soldiers all around, I even forgot we were at war. At the top of a small rise I could see that the earth had turned green. Apple trees blossomed, bluebirds and brown thrashers sang their songs, and crows darted in and out of furrows of corn that were just beginning to sprout.

When we got back to Father's company, the men were serious and full of activity.

They were getting ready for battle.

CHAPTER NINE

Preparing for Battle

Father's company had orders to report to Cambridge Common at six o'clock with one day's worth of food and drink. His fellow soldiers had spent the afternoon molding musket balls out of chunks of lead.

"How many Redcoats will you be killing?" Father's captain asked me.

I gulped.

He laughed at my nervousness, but the other men began teasing, urging me to stay and fight.

"You want to be there to help us beat the Redcoats, don't you, boy?"

"We'll send them running, like the Patriots did at Concord and Lexington," another man said.

Father listened with a smile on his face. Did he want me to stay? I didn't want him to think me a coward.

"I'd like to stay," I told Father. "I won't make it back to the Neck by nightfall, and it's not safe to travel after dark," I said. "Mother won't be expecting me before tomorrow evening."

The men cheered, but worry ate at my stomach. I tried to tell myself that I would not be scared of the fighting with Father at my side.

"Whatever lies ahead isn't work for a boy," he answered. "You can stay in Cambridge tonight and go back to Boston in the morning."

The fear drained out of me and I nodded. If Father said I couldn't fight, I couldn't fight. There would be no shame in my leaving.

"We may have need of a messenger," the captain said. "Someone to run information back to headquarters."

The men watched with interested faces. Father looked at me long and hard. He sized me up, measuring my ability to carry out my duties. I said nothing, my fear mixed with pride that he might consider me almost a man.

"Mind that you take cover at the first sign of fire," he told me.

The men around us cheered again. One or two slapped me on the back. I pretended to cheer with them.

"Mayhap we'll enter Boston together tomorrow," Father said.

"On the heels of the Redcoats as they flee to their ships," the captain added.

The men cheered at the thought. "Huzzah! Huzzah!"

There was no time for my fear to grow. Quickly we bedded Star down in a farmer's barn. I patted her nose and hoped she would be far away from the sounds of war. Then I raced back to the Common to take my place with the soldiers.

After a long and fervent prayer led by the Reverend Mr. Langdon, the president of Harvard College, we commenced to march. Our destination was still a mystery. We had been warned to keep silent, but the earth rumbled with the sounds of hundreds of marching feet. I heard a horse whinny and soon was passed by a cart carrying tools for digging.

I caught Father's eye and he nodded at me. It was a glorious thing to be a part of such a group. I knew that tomorrow I would have to make my way back to Boston, but for now I was a soldier.

Our leaders were General Israel Putnam—Old Put—from Connecticut and Colonel William Prescott from Groton. Father told me he was no relation, Prescott being a fairly common name in New England, but still I took pride in the fact that a Prescott was a colonel. I was sure he was a better one than Stockdale.

We crossed the narrow Charlestown Neck with the Mystic River on our left and the Charles on our right. Then I knew our aim—we would take the hills of the Charlestown peninsula before the British could do the same! I chuckled at the fact that the Redcoats expected no such thing. We had outsmarted them, and my information had helped.

When we reached the lower slope of Bunker's Hill, we rested, still silent. I drank from my canteen and wished I had slipped some food into my pockets. My stomach growled.

I heard a muffled dispute. Father was called to the front, and I marched with him. The officers debated as to which of Charlestown's hills should be fortified. The orders read Bunker's Hill, by far the tallest of the hills, but Breed's Hill was closer to Boston and to the shipping.

"It's better suited to a battle," Old Put declared.

"The orders are for Bunker's Hill," Colonel Prescott insisted. "Surely we need to follow orders."

Father assured them that because a ridge ran between the two hills, Breed's was often lumped in with Bunker's Hill. That decided the matter. Colonel Prescott relented, and we were on the march again, over the ridge and to the top of Breed's Hill.

The moon was a mere sliver, but the night was bright with stars. I set to digging with the rest of the men. The earth was soft and scarcely stony. British warships sat in the waters between Charlestown and Boston. Their bells rang out every half hour, and we heard the cry of "all's well" from the sentries on board. The only other sound was the occasional click of pick against rock as we silently built a fortification that would surprise the Redcoats at daybreak.

At some point I curled up and fell asleep. I woke to discover a fort with dirt walls taller than Father and as thick as the length of a bayonet. A deep ditch surrounded the fortification, save where my carcass lay. The men had worked around me. Now I shook the sleep from my eyes and grabbed my shovel to finish the task. Platforms of wood and earth were built inside the walls to stand upon when it was time to fire on the enemy.

At dawn, the HMS *Lively* was the first to notice we had seized the hill. Her ten big guns opened up, firing cannonballs in our direction. I hit the ground in an instant, sure that I would lose my life at any moment. Men crouched around me, then stood with nervous laughs when they realized that the balls only hit the side of the hill.

Father helped me to my feet. "There's no shame in your going back to Cambridge. I think you'd better leave now."

I shook my head and forced a shaky smile before picking up my shovel again. "I want to stay."

Old Put looked through his spyglass and laughed at the shocked expression on the captain's face. "We've fooled them, men!" he shouted. "Keep your heads down and dig! By the time they get their soldiers out of bed, we'll have six forts built!"

"Huzzah!" The soldiers were tired and hungry, but they kept working.

Soon the HMS *Somerset* and other ships in the squadron joined the warship *Lively*, along with a battery of six British guns atop Copp's Hill. Cannonball after cannonball pounded into the side of Breed's Hill and our fort. I'd never seen such a storm of round shot as was poured onto us, but our fort stood undamaged.

I joined in the cheers of the soldiers around me each time we heard the thud of a ball hitting the strong dirt walls and then rolling back down the hill. Then one soldier became too bold. A private stood tall and raised his arms in the air. The next I saw, his head was gone. I jumped to avoid the smoking six-pound ball that rolled past my feet.

I was ready to bolt like Star on Boston Neck. My stomach heaved, but there was nothing to bring up. I swallowed hard and forced myself to keep breathing. The thud of balls continued. Pounding. One after the next. The crush of bodies around me made it impossible to run.

Men panicked. Some ran back toward the Charlestown Neck. Others talked of leaving. They had worked all night, one argued; it was time for reinforcements to take over. They had no food, no drink. How could they be expected to fight?

I could not find Father in the crowd.

Colonel Prescott suddenly jumped on top of the parapet surrounding the fort and strolled back and forth. He pretended to inspect the work, but really he was calming the men. Another joined him, seeing his aim. It was Father. He strolled along the parapet as if he was looking for a pleasant resting place along the Charles on a summer's day. My heart stopped beating with each ball that thudded into the hill, but none came close to Father or to the colonel.

Their coolness quieted everyone's nerves. The men buried the body. We took off our hats while another soldier said a few words over the grave. Soon the soldiers were once again cheering with each shot.

I gritted my teeth. I had never seen violent death up close before, and I wondered at their ability to forget so quickly. But soon my voice joined theirs again.

"Huzzah!"

CHAPTER TEN

Charlestown Burns

By eleven o'clock we had done all we could. The fortification was as strong as it would ever be. Then we waited. It was only when the dust finally settled that I became aware of my powerful thirst, but there was no water to be had, nor any food.

The sun was a furious, fiery ball above us. None could remember a day as hot as this. Sweat and dirt made my eyes sting, and my head ached. I closed my eyes for a moment and in seconds I was swimming in the cool water of the Charles. Then a ball pounded into the wall and startled me awake. Father was beside me.

"Daniel, I want you to move back to Bunker's Hill," he said quietly, indicating the taller hill behind us. "Some men are building another fortification. If we're forced to retreat, we'll have need of it."

"Will you come?" I asked. I was relieved to be moving away from the cannonballs, but I did not want to be away from Father.

He shook his head and pointed toward the Mystic River. Old Put and a small company of men were frantically throwing up a fort along an old rail fence. "That's where I'll be," he said. He put his hands on my shoulders and leaned in so that we were nose-to-nose. "Listen very carefully."

I nodded.

"If the Redcoats come close, I want you to run." His eyes flicked to the shallow grave of the headless man and then back to me.

I tried to swallow, but my mouth was too dry.

"If a British soldier—even one—breaches this fort, run as fast as you can. Don't stop until you're on the far side of the Charlestown Neck and on your way to Cambridge. Do not look for me. Do not wait for me," he said. "Run."

Fear mixed with gravity in his eyes. I saw my own eyes, wide with alarm, reflected in his. I didn't care that we stood surrounded by soldiers and that I had pretended to be a man among them. I hugged him.

I hugged Father like a boy. He held me for a moment and patted my shoulder while he whispered of his pride in me. I didn't deserve his praise, but I allowed him to soothe me the way I had soothed Star on Boston Neck.

Then we parted. Father strode to the rail fence. I ran to the top of Bunker's Hill. When I reached the summit, I saw a fever of activity in Boston's streets. The town's rooftops were dense with onlookers waiting to view the battle. Redcoats marched toward North Battery. Sailors were ready to row them across the water. Other barges came round the tip of the peninsula, probably from Long Wharf. Below me, Charlestown smoldered. The citizens had all fled, and the cannonballs sent wisps of smoke into the sky.

It was near noon when one by one the boats pushed out, a scarlet mass of soldiers in each of them. They landed near Morton's Hill. A captain allowed me to look through his spyglass, and I watched the Redcoats settle down in neat rows with their packs and seem to eat a meal.

Dread filled my stomach in place of food.

"Back to work, men," a captain shouted.

My arms quivered with fatigue, but I picked up my shovel again and commenced to dig. Reinforcements from New Hampshire arrived and joined Old Put and Father on the army's flank.

It was another two hours before the British made their move.

A solid line of scarlet climbed Breed's Hill, a bloody river running in the wrong direction. Wave after wave of Redcoats walked through grass to their knees, crossing fences and stepping over holes in a slow, steady advance.

My hands gripped my shovel. Our men were quiet, waiting. Old Put roared in the tense silence, "Don't fire until you see the whites of their eyes." There was no gunpowder to spare.

The Redcoats seemed to be upon the very walls of the fort. The soldier next to me muttered a prayer. Would our men not stand and fight? I remembered my promise to Father and steeled myself to run.

Suddenly the Patriots let loose with a burst of fire. Smoke boiled in all directions. The first wave of Redcoats fell. And then the next, and the next. Suddenly the British were running helter-skelter down the hill. The river had turned and flowed in the other direction.

I cheered until I was hoarse. A man beside me patted me on the back as if I was one of them, and suddenly I realized that I was. I threw my shoulders back and stood tall. The Patriot soldiers, the men that Stockdale mocked as a "preposterous parade," had made the mighty Redcoats scurry away like rats. And I was a Patriot, too.

When the smoke cleared, I saw just how many bodies they had left behind. Redcoats dotted the hill. Some crawled. Most were still. Few in the Patriot fort appeared to be wounded. I saw one man tie a bandage around his arm and then raise his musket in triumph amid great cheers.

Our triumph was not to last.

The captain raised his spyglass. "They're regrouping."

★ CHAPTER ELEVEN ★

The Battle of Bunker's Hill

The Redcoats were indeed getting ready for another attack. Drums rattled to call them to formation.

A Patriot captain tried to urge some of the men forward. Few followed him as he raced to reinforce those at the front on Breed's Hill.

A crimson line formed at the bottom of the hill. They stepped over the bodies of their own as if they were just one more fence to be surmounted.

A man stood by my side, a fisherman from the looks of him. "Those men will surely die today," he said, pointing to the left flank where Father stood with Old Put.

Fear surged through me. Father was going to be

attacked from two fronts. Redcoats marched toward him and a warship sailed up the Mystic River. Its cannons crashed like thunder. The Patriots' cannons were no match for the ship's big guns. I narrowed my eyes and used my hands to block out the fierce sun, but I could not make out Father in the crush of men.

A breeze, the first I had felt all day, carried with it the moans of the wounded Redcoats on Breed's Hill. They begged for help, but their fellow soldiers were fixed on the fort at the top of the slope.

Charlestown was ablaze behind them. The church steeple formed a great pyramid of fire above the town before it fell. One by one chimneys crumbled, sending up towers of sparks.

The Redcoats advanced, their steps in perfect unison.

This time our men waited even longer before they commenced to fight. The Redcoats seemed impossibly close to the walls of the fort before there was a burst of fire and smoke and noise. The first wave of Redcoats fell, and then the second. An officer waved a sword in the air to urge the soldiers forward. A third wave began to fall and once again the king's men turned and ran. A good many of them were left behind, broken or dead.

I begged for the loan of a spyglass. Old Put's men

were grouped around something—or someone. I searched for Father but could not make him out. Was he at the center of that group, broken like the British on the hill? Finally, I saw him. There was blood on his breeches. His own or someone else's? My heart pounded and I held my breath as I moved the glass up and down, checking every limb. With great relief I saw that he appeared to be unhurt.

Such a long time passed after the second attack that we began to believe the Redcoats might give up on the notion of a third. Then we saw more soldiers sailing from Boston—fresh reinforcements. Our own men were far from fresh. They had no food, no water, no sleep. They were almost out of powder.

The Redcoats changed tactics for their third advance up the hill. Instead of long, wide lines, they formed three columns. I saw that columns would be harder to scatter. They were almost upon the fort again before our men commenced to shoot. But this time there was no big volley of fire and smoke—the Patriots were completely out of gunpowder. The Redcoats wavered for an instant, and then sprang forward.

The fortunes of the day were suddenly reversed. The first Redcoat mounted the parapet and leaped into the fort. Soon they stormed in from three sides.

The Patriots used their muskets as clubs, but they were no match for British bayonets. Dust rose in clouds. Our men were now the ones to retreat. They fled in all directions.

Father had told me to run, but I tarried, looking for him among the men streaming toward us from the rail fence. Something drew my attention back to Breed's Hill, and my eyes settled on a man about the same height as Father. It was Dr. Warren. The men had cheered that morning when he arrived and took his place among them. Now he defended an exit, making it possible for many of the Patriots to escape. He was one of the last to retreat. Then he stopped and turned, perhaps for one last stand. I saw a bullet strike his head. Dr. Warren fell.

Men streamed around me, racing down the hill. I knew I should join them, but my eyes were fixed on Dr. Warren. I willed him to stand and run. But even from my distance, I could see that he was dead.

Someone grabbed my arm and pulled me along. We bolted down Bunker's Hill. To my left a man tripped and fell, rolling like a giant shooter in a game of marbles. He knocked others out of his path as if they were mere toys.

Now the same ship that threatened Father earlier shot at me as I retreated across Charlestown Neck. I did not stop running until I reached Ploughed Hill, near Cambridge.

Old Put was once again throwing up a fortification in case the Redcoats tried to chase us all the way to Cambridge. I flopped on the ground to catch my breath, holding my side. Father found me there.

I did not know how frightened I was until I saw him. I buried my head in his shoulder and wept. My emotions were in an uproar. Father was alive, but many were dead, and the British might still be on our heels.

"Daniel," he said, running his hands over my body. "Are you hurt?"

It was only then that I noticed my shirt was splattered with blood. Whose? I wondered. "No," I answered, struggling to sit up. "I'm not hurt."

Two wounded men hobbled past us, one with a gaping wound in his neck, the other with a gash in his leg. I closed my eyes so that I would not have to see them.

"Do you think you can make it to Star?" Father asked. "Ask the farmer if you can hitch her to a cart. The wounded need help getting to Cambridge."

"What if the Redcoats . . ." my voice trailed off. I didn't want to help the wounded; I didn't even want to look at them, but I was ashamed to say as much.

"Daniel, these men need us," he said. "Some can't walk."

Someone moaned and I shuddered.

"The Redcoats won't come this far, not tonight,"

Father said. He waved at the half-built fort. "This is simply a safeguard."

I nodded and stood. A great weariness had come over me, but I trod forward, putting one foot in front of the other. My eyes were fixed on the ground, avoiding the men around me. Everywhere was terror and confusion. The day's fortunes had turned so suddenly, and the soldiers were disheartened by their loss. I heard some say that the battle would have been ours, if not for the want of powder.

Finally, I reached Cambridge and the barn. Star nuzzled me and I buried my face in her neck, drinking in her rich horse smell and trying to clear my nose of the reek of blood and fear and fire.

I had not eaten a mouthful of victuals in twenty-four hours. The farmer's wife gave me a meat pie and a firkin of cider to wash it down with, along with the use of a cart.

I hitched Star to the cart and set off for Ploughed Hill. I did not want to go back and help the wounded, but I had promised Father. I passed the Common at Cambridge. It was already filled with wounded soldiers, and Dr. Church had set up a kind of hospital. Men limped toward me. Those who could walk were not my charges. I pressed on.

I found a man kneeling by the side of the road, moaning. I jumped off the cart to help him. Star's nostrils flared and her ears were pinned back. I kept one hand on her while I stepped nearer. Someone had bandaged his wounds, but he was still bleeding fiercely. He opened his eyes, but did not see me.

"It's dark," he said.

I kneeled next to him.

He slumped over and fell into me. Dead.

I pushed him off and jumped to my feet. The cider and meat pie rushed up from my stomach and splattered the ground. Tears streamed down my face. I wanted to be quit of war. Quit of blood. Quit of death.

There was just enough time to get to Boston before dark. I did not mind Father. I did not look for wounded to cart to the hospital. I unhitched the cart and left the dead man where he lay; I turned Star around and flew through Cambridge. Star was unflagging as we galloped through Brookline and Roxbury, refusing to stop and share news of the battle. I said as little as possible to the guards at the American lines— Father had secured me a pass the day before—and raced toward Boston Neck and home.

CHAPTER TWELVE

"Those cursed rebels, they would not flinch."

I let Star take the lead, and she was as happy to run from the war as I was. She was in a full lather when we reached the Redcoat fortifications at the town gate. I handed over the pass with shaking hands.

The sentries were not the same as the ones I had encountered when I left Boston. It was a wonder to me that only three days had passed. The time felt much longer.

One sentry ran his eyes up and down my person, taking in the dirt on my breeches. My coat covered the blood on my shirt, but not that on my hands. I tried to hide it, but it was too late. Why had I not thought to stop and wash?

"Get down," he ordered.

Star commenced to snort and dance. I did as the guard said, trying to soothe the horse at the same time.

Two sentries held their muskets on me while the third searched my person.

Once the soldiers satisfied themselves that I carried no guns or powder, they turned their attention to me.

"Where did the blood come from?" one of them asked. "Were you among the fighting?"

"I came upon a wounded man on the side of the road. I tried to help him." My brain formed a picture of the soldier I had watched crumple over to his death. "But he died." I could only whisper the last words.

My horror was real enough for them. Their leader, a sergeant, patted my shoulder. As he did I heard the paper I carried in my waistcoat rustle. I had forgotten about the other pass—the Patriot pass. If the guards found it would they arrest me? Star sensed my fear. Her neck stiffened and she began to dance again, but the sentry only handed me my coat and waved me through.

I rode Star through Boston. Wounded Redcoats limped in the streets. Smoke continued to rise over

Charlestown. All around were tight clumps of Loyalists and soldiers gossiping about the day. I had no wish to listen to stories. I imagined their disgust if they learned of my shameful behavior. People on both sides of the war had the right to call me a coward. How many wounded struggled alone while I ran away? I wanted to shut them out. To be safe in Mother's kitchen, or to curl up next to her in bed the way I did when I was Sarah's age.

First there was work to be done. I stopped to wash the blood off my hands so as not to alarm Mother and Sarah. There was naught I could do about my shirt except make sure my coat covered the stains.

My heart jumped in my chest when I came to our tavern. The wooden sign with its blue whale creaked in the breeze, and the front door stood open to let in the early evening air. I bedded Star down in the stable, giving her extra oats and hay, despite the grumbling of the soldier who took care of Colonel Stockdale's and the other officers' horses. Star had worked hard, and it had been a long time since I was able to reward her with a carrot or an apple.

Sarah heard me and ran out into the yard. "There was a bad-dle," she said. "Big, big booms!"

Concern filled her little face. I could hardly remember a time before soldiers. She had known nothing else in her short life. It was me she turned to when the boom of the cannon scared her. And I hadn't been there. I had failed everyone today.

"I heard them," I told her, shaking off my dark thoughts. "I was very afraid. And you weren't there to pet me and tell me to be brave."

That drew a smile from her. Then I remembered the maple sugar candy one of Father's friends had given to me in camp. It was in my pocket.

"Do you know any little girls who might like some maple sugar candy?"

"Me! Me!" She hopped like a bunny, giggling.

"I think, mayhap, I have some in my pockets."

She squealed with delight when she found her prize.

Mother stood at the back door watching us, wiping her hands on her apron. Her eyes were bright, and she looked tired and scared. I hadn't given a thought to how worried Mother would be. Tears filled my own eyes. I wanted to throw myself in her arms and cry out my whole story.

I could not.

Aunt Abigail suddenly appeared behind Mother and started to wail. "Where are my boys? Where are my boys?"

"Safe," I told her. "They did not take part in the battle, but they would not return with me."

That seemed to satisfy her. She was quiet long enough to allow Mother to ask a question.

"And the Andersons in Salem, did you see them?" she asked.

That was code for Father. I nodded. "I did. They are well. They miss their friends in Boston."

Mother's face crumpled a bit, but she was mindful of Colonel Stockdale's soldier in the stable. "I was worried about all of you today. There was fighting in Charlestown and beyond."

My eyes locked on hers. I wanted to tell her what I had done and what I had seen. I wanted the comfort she would give, and even the scolding that would surely come when she discovered I had put myself in harm's way. But to tell her would only bring her more worry.

Mother pulled at the hem of my shirt, and then opened my jacket. Her knees buckled when she saw the blood. Aunt Abigail screamed.

"I came across an injured man on the side of the road and tried to help him. But I stayed clear of the fighting," I lied. "So did the Andersons."

Mother's eyes jumped from me to Sarah and back to me. "I am glad of that," she said weakly.

I don't think she believed me, but she didn't want to frighten Sarah, or alert anyone about the tavern that I had been among the fighting.

Sarah threw herself at me again, searching for more candy. She was rewarded with one last piece.

When I had left the Patriots, they were disheartened by their defeat. But I quickly learned that the British were just as discouraged. The officers who gathered in the tavern were glum indeed. The Redcoats might have possession of Bunker's Hill, but the price they paid for the land in British lives was much too high.

I wished I could use that information to mock them, to get back at Stockdale and the others for all the times they had scoffed at the Patriots. The army they called ridiculous had sent them running down Breed's Hill—twice!—and had only been defeated in the end because they ran out of gunpowder. The might of the British army could not stand against strong New England men.

A cascade of bleeding Redcoats had crossed the Charles River back into Boston, and the slopes of Breed's Hill were covered with the graves of slain Englishmen. It was said that General Howe's entire staff was killed or wounded.

Our own Captain Smythe and Lieutenant Johnson would not return from the battle.

Many of the wounded who had been ferried back to Boston died. The next day I passed more dead men in the streets than live ones. At every corner I came upon a funeral march or an auction for the property of one officer or another. The chapel bells rang almost all day for Redcoats who had died from their wounds. It was so melancholy that General Gage put a stop to the tolling of the bells for funerals.

I wondered how many of the Patriot wounded had died before they made it back to Cambridge. Could I have saved one soldier? Two?

Colonel Stockdale survived. He walked into the tavern after camping on the hill for two nights, his breeches splattered with blood, and ordered a glass of rum.

"Those cursed rebels, they would not flinch."

★ CHAPTER THIRTEEN ★

Salt Pork and Beans

July, 1775

As soon as I could, I turned the boot scraper around to signal a meeting with Master Richardson. I had no intelligence to share, but I wanted Father to know that I had arrived home safely.

I waited at the pump the next morning, and the next. I thought perhaps he was on a mission to the Patriot camp, but on Wednesday afternoon I spied the schoolmaster in front of the Province House, General Gage's home and headquarters. He was in the company of Mr. Henshaw and some officers. I wondered why his tutoring duties would bring him into such close contact with the Redcoats, and his countenance gave me a momentary worry. He appeared happy to be among them. Then he saw me and gave me a nod and wink. No doubt he was gathering important information for the Patriots.

The next morning, he came.

"Mr. Henshaw keeps me very busy," Master Richardson explained. "I continue to tutor Josiah, and act as secretary to Mr. Henshaw himself."

"Are you learning much of value?" I asked.

He nodded, but said no more. He was also silent when I asked him how he was able to slip in and out of Boston so easily.

"It's not safe for you to know," he told me.

As soon as he learned that I had been at Bunker's Hill for the fighting, however, he peppered me with questions.

I had tried not to let my mind settle on the battle and what I had done afterward. Some visited the Patriot soldiers who had been taken prisoner by the Redcoats during the battle, but I was too ashamed. At night when I went to bed, pictures flitted across my brain. I would see Dr. Warren fall, or hear Old Put yell for powder, or feel the weight of the dead soldier as he slumped into me. A deep shame burned in my stomach when I remembered running away.

The images flooded back with Master Richardson's questions. I set down my yoke and buckets. My story poured out of me like water from the pump. I told him of the dirt and the noise, the fear and the confusion.

The schoolmaster was a careful listener. He put a hand on my shoulder to comfort me, and I found myself confessing that I had run away with Star when there were wounded who needed my aid. It helped me somewhat to talk, but Master Richardson quickly moved to more practical matters. He had many questions I could not answer.

He wanted to know about the Patriots' stores of powder and their guns. He asked for my opinion of Colonel Prescott and General Putnam, and of how they had fared under the stress of battle. Most of all, he wanted information about the Patriots' spy network.

"There are others who provide intelligence. It's said that General Gage has a mole in his very office. Have you heard any names?" he asked.

I could not satisfy his curiosity, and I found his questions peculiar. Was it not Master Richardson who had made clear to me the value of keeping such things secret? Then he explained himself.

"I will soon go to camp, but I may not return—not until we drive these wretched Redcoats from Boston. There are some who suspect where my true loyalties lie," he said. "I will have to find another to convey your intelligence to General Ward."

He lifted the yoke and helped me balance it on my shoulders. "I will come to you before I leave and give you the name of a man you can trust," he promised.

I walked away slowly, careful not to spill my water buckets. I had taken great comfort in the fact that my schoolmaster was close by. I wondered if I would have the courage to continue my work without him. Could I trust someone else?

The first person I saw upon leaving the schoolmaster was one in whom I could not trust, of that I had no doubt. Josiah Henshaw marched down the street rattling on a drum.

"Prescott!" he yelled, "don't you have a black boy to tote your water?"

I glared at him. My father didn't hold with slavery and neither did I.

"Mayhap my father will employ you," he snickered. "One of our slaves has run off to join the rebels and we have need of a simpleton."

"There's much work to do at the tavern," I said, pushing past him. "I have no time for children's games." I eyed his drum with a sneer.

"I'm only teasing," he said. "And this isn't a toy. I'm a soldier." He threw his shoulders back and drummed a quick parade step. "Loyal volunteers have formed a company in case the rebels attack, and Father signed me up to be a drummer. We'll drive them out of Massachusetts in no time. We're to drill every day."

"What of your lessons with Master Richardson?" I asked.

"Hah! I finished with lessons the day those rebel fools started this war," he said. "As soon as we've ended it, I'm to go into business with my father. No more schooling and games for me."

I knew him to be lying. Master Richardson continued his lessons with Josiah. He told me so. I could not let on what I knew. Nor could I tell Josiah that the Patriots would be the victors, not the Redcoats. I look my leave of him and continued on my way.

Master Richardson slipped out of Boston two weeks later. He gave me the name of a barber—a Mr. Newell—who was said to travel back and forth from camp to town.

The war remained at a standstill, with cannonading and small skirmishes, but no more battles. Colonel Stockdale and others wanted to attack the Patriots, but "Grandma Gage" waited for reinforcements from England. The siege of Boston continued.

In midsummer we learned that the Continental Congress in Philadelphia had appointed a new commander for the army. George Washington, from the Virginia colony, was said to have fought at Gage's side in the war with the French and the Indians. Now Washington would fight against Gage.

The Redcoats in our tavern heaped indignities upon the people of Boston, and all Mother and I could do was stand by in silence and keep serving them.

One hot summer evening our hired soldier could not be with us. Mother and I had run back and forth with plates of food, but the meal was finally over and I manned the tap while Mother cleaned up. As usual, the soldiers played at their cards and dice, while others sang drinking songs.

One of them stood and minced across the floor. "I'm Dr. Warren," he said in a high womanly voice, "and I'll lead my rebel soldiers to—" Suddenly he fell to the floor as if he were dead.

The men pounded the tables in approval. Stockdale roared with laughter.

Others joined the man in his playacting. Some took off their coats and cowered and whimpered, begging for their lives. "Long live the king!" one of them cried. "And please save my sorry rebellious hide." Redcoats pretended to be about to stab them with bayonets.

Stockdale's big meaty fist hammered against his table. "Kill the sorry cowards! Kill them!" he chanted.

One soldier pretended to be a Patriot and begged

for his life. "Please, I've been led astray," he moaned. "I'm a king's man now."

"Kill the rebel! Kill the rebel!" Stockdale shouted with a grin.

I watched the spittle fly from his lip and gripped a tankard. How I wanted to throw it at him. How dare they mock the death of a great man like Dr. Warren? How dare they portray the Patriot soldiers as sniveling cowards? I had seen them at Breed's Hill, and they fought bravely until the end.

I forced myself to fill the tankard and set it on the bar. The charade was over in a moment. Soon they were back at their cards and dice. Those who were not otherwise engaged bawled a drinking song.

At least when they were in the tavern they could not bring harm to others. As the siege continued, law-abiding Patriots were thrown in jail and kept there for silly offenses. Liberty Tree—the grand old elm where the Sons of Liberty had met and plotted—was chopped down for firewood.

It seemed as if half the town had smallpox, a nasty disease that killed most who came down with it and left the rest pitted with horrible scars. Food continued to be dear, even food for Star. I was forced to sell her to an officer for a few coins.

"She'll do for an exercise horse," he said with a sneer.

I patted Star's neck and buried my face in it so that she would not feel the insult. Then I reluctantly handed over the reins. I heard her whinny as I walked away, but I could not bear to look back at her. Tears streamed down my face as I trudged home.

In August, a notice was posted saying those who wished to leave Boston could apply for permission at the Province House. Mother and I whispered about it. She and I had both been inoculated with the small-pox, but Sarah had not. We were desperate to protect her. Aunt Abigail intended to take her family to our cousins in Marblehead.

"Perhaps we should go with her," Mother said.

It was decided I should seek Father's advice. Two days later, I boarded one of the few fishing boats with a pass to leave the town. The pass was for four men, but only three would be fishing. I would disembark to visit the Patriot camp.

CHAPTER FOURTEEN

Wild Men and General Washington

August, 1775

The fishing boat captain rowed to shore near the road to Lynn. It was just after dawn. "Be back by four o'clock or it will be all our heads," he warned me. His pass was for four fishermen. He could not return with less.

I set off on a slow, steady run to Cambridge. The day quickly became hot and sticky, but I dared not take off my coat for fear I'd lose it. Mother had replaced my buttons with cloth-covered coins for Father. I crossed the Mystic at a spot where the water was low and felt some relief from the heat. There was a time when I could take a swim on a hot summer day without worry. Now I had too much work to do in the tavern, or a mission to fulfill like today. I wondered if I would ever have such freedom again.

I came to Winter Hill and was suddenly ordered to halt by three men who appeared as if by witch-craft. From their clothing I took them to be Indians, but their skin was white. All three of them wore fringed deerskin shirts and had tomahawks tied to their belts.

"State your business," one of them demanded. He eyed me from behind a musket such as I had never seen—it had a long, skinny barrel.

I raised my hands to show them I was unarmed and prayed they would not shoot. "Dan-Dan-Daniel Prescott," I stuttered. "I'm . . . I'm going to see my father at Cambridge—a soldier."

The men lowered their guns and after many questions gave me leave to go.

Now I was spooked by every shadow, and I jump-ed when a squirrel crossed my path. But I made it to Cambridge without any further assaults on my person.

The camp was much changed. It had more of a military look about it. The men's uniforms were still a mixture of this and that, but they marched more smartly.

There were more flags about than there had been when I was here last. Many companies flew the British

Union Jack. I also saw the New England pine tree flag with the motto AN APPEAL TO HEAVEN. Other banners stated what the men fought for—LIBERTY. And I spotted more than one flag with a rattlesnake coiled and ready to strike over the words DON'T TREAD ON ME.

As soon as the wind blew from the west I could tell where the necessaries were, but they were no longer scattered about higgledy-piggledy. I went to the area where Father's company had been camped, only to find another in its place.

I asked where they were. There was such a flurry of response, each man talking over the next, that I could not make it out. Later I learned that the men were from New York, and that all New Yorkers talk loudly and all together, breaking in on you whenever they have a notion. Finally a captain from Rhode Island came to my aid with language I could understand and pointed me to Cambridge.

"They've been taken up by His Excellency—General Washington," he told me.

"General Washington?" I asked.

"They're guards at headquarters. His Excellency needs men he can trust about him." I beamed with pride. Father was a man General Washington trusted! I found him outside the general's headquarters, his musket at the ready. My stomach lurched when I saw him. What if he had heard about my cowardly behavior after the battle? Was he ashamed of me? Would he want to see me? Then Father turned. His eyes drank me in like cold water on a hot summer's day, and I felt my heart squeeze.

Remembering the alarm on his face the last time I visited, I was quick to inform him that all was well. He did not ask me about what happened after the battle, and I held my tongue. Instead I shared Mother's concerns, and asked about leaving Boston.

"We have fever here in camp," Father said when I told him about the smallpox in town. "It's begun to spread to the countryside. Sarah will be in just as much danger outside the town—perhaps more."

My heart sank at his answer. I didn't know until that moment how weary I was of life in Boston. "We don't know when food will become scarce again," I told him. "I am happy that the Patriots have been able to capture so many British supply ships, but the people of Boston will starve along with the Redcoats."

"Colonel Stockdale isn't such a blackguard that he'll let you starve," Father said. "But his men will plunder the tavern if you leave. We would have nothing to return to after the war."

"Will it end soon, do you think?" I asked him.

He nodded. "General Washington is a fine military man. It won't be too much longer before we drive the British out—or King George agrees to grant our demands."

I wondered if the Patriots had the strength to attack the British. I was about to ask Father when Old Put emerged from the house General Washington used as his headquarters.

"Powder!" he yelled. "If not for this want of powder."

A man I took to be General Washington stood behind him with a grave expression. He was tall and of strong build, with a handsome face and intelligent eyes. He wore a proper uniform with a sash and a saber at his side. He looked grand. His eyes fell to me. "Is this the young spy I've been hearing about, Prescott?" he asked.

"Aye, sir," Father answered.

I heard the pride in Father's voice. I straightened my shoulders and stretched as tall as I possibly could.

"How did you get to us today?" he asked.

"A fishing boat, sir. We landed near the road to Lynn, and I ran from there."

"Do you return to Boston today?" he asked.

"Yes, sir."

"And when you're serving ale and rum, do you ever talk to the officers?"

"Sometimes, sir," I said, growing alarmed. Did the general think I was a spy for the Redcoats? "I have to."

"That's fine, of course you must." He nodded thoughtfully and commenced to walk away with Old Put. Then he stopped and turned to me again. "The next time you have the opportunity, can you share a rumor about our powder?"

"Your gunpowder?"

"Yes." A slow smile spread across General Washington's face. "Tell the British that you heard we have so much gunpowder, eighteen hundred barrels worth, that we don't know what to do with it all. Can you do that, Daniel?"

"Yes, sir!" I said.

"Thank you, Daniel."

Father put his hand on my shoulder, and we watched the general walk away.

"Do you still want to leave Boston?" Father asked.

"No," I told him. "Not if I can help the general."

I was still marveling at the general's kindness when I sensed someone come up behind us. I turned to find Master Richardson looking puzzled. He had a quill in his hand and his fingers were ink stained. I thought my schoolmaster would be pleased to see me, but like Father, his first thought was one of concern.

"What are you doing here?" he asked. "You're supposed to pass your information to barber Newell, not come yourself."

"I needed to speak to Father," I said.

"And a good thing he came. General Washington has a mission for Daniel," Father said.

The schoolmaster was plainly curious. "A mission?"

I nodded, but I thought it best not to share my secret. Nor did Father. We were ill at ease in the silence.

"Master Richardson is a secretary to Dr. Church," Father said.

I babbled, pleased to have something to fill the silence. "It must be more enjoyable than working for Mr. Henshaw and tutoring Josiah," I said.

"Mr. Henshaw?" Father asked.

The schoolmaster stiffened. His knuckles were white where he gripped the quill. "I worked for the Henshaws before I left Boston. I saw an opportunity to help our cause and put food in my stomach, and I took it." He turned to me. "Will you be able to carry out your mission, Daniel? I recall that you sometimes have had trouble with that."

My face burned. Master Richardson knew of two instances when I had behaved like a coward. Had he told Father? Would he tell General Washington?

"I'm sure Daniel will do his best," Father said.

Father's watch ended then and his relief arrived, putting an end to our awkward meeting.

Suddenly it was time for me to leave. Father quickly removed the cloth-covered coins that served as my buttons. There was no time to replace the coins with buttonmolds, but who would notice missing buttons on a boy's coat? Father walked me as far as Prospect Hill. Along the way he explained the strange men I had met that morning.

"Backwoodsmen from Virginia and Pennsylvania. Hunters," he said. "They're a curious, wild lot. They live off the land. Those rifles carry bullets farther than any musket I've ever seen, and they have expert aim."

"Whose side are they on?" I asked.

Father chuckled. "Their own, mostly, but they're Patriots." He continued with a warning. "Don't run if you see them again, or you'll surely end up with a bullet in your back."

I assured him I would not. I had to bid farewell before I could ask him about my schoolmaster's odd behavior. I also wondered when I would see Father again. But foremost on my mind was the fear of running into more of those woodsmen.

"Give Mother and Sarah my love," he said.

I promised I would.

"And don't forget your mission."

I smiled. "Wait until Grandma Gage hears about the powder," I said. "He might leave Boston without any fight at all."

★ CHAPTER FIFTEEN ★

A Mission for the General

Iwalked all the way to the spot where I was to meet the fishing boat without coming upon any more wild men. I arrived before my time, and my wait was a lengthy one. When the sun in the sky indicated that it was well past four o'clock, I began to fret. What if they forgot me and I had to find another way back to Boston? I waited and waited. At last they came.

The fishing had been good. The boat's hold was full of cod and mackerel. I was given some of each to bring back to the tavern. Mother roasted one whole fish just for the colonel. I was happy enough with the watery fish stew and the fish pies that would last the rest of us for many days. I was more interested in carrying out my mission for General Washington. I hoped I could make up for my cowardly behavior at Breed's Hill.

The next night and the one after, Colonel Stockdale dined out. Finally he ate at home. Our hired soldier was not in, so I manned the tap.

"Ale, sir?" I asked him.

"Rum," he grunted.

The colonel was in a foul mood, but no more than usual. I often avoided speaking to him, but today I would try to draw him out the way Father used to.

"How goes the war?" I asked.

He only grunted.

I grabbed a rag and wiped imaginary spills. "Do you think General Gage will force the rebels away before winter? It'll be a hungry one if not," I said, trying to be conversational.

Stockdale downed his rum and banged on the bar to signal he wanted more.

I tried again. "The rebels are well armed, I believe."

"The rebels are farmers and fisherman. Their weapons are as preposterous as they are," Stockdale spat. "And yet Gage waits for reinforcements." He shook his head, clearly believing that the wait was unnecessary. "One strong blow is all we need. We'll conquer them sure. If Gage won't, Howe will."

My ears perked up. Was Gage leaving? I kept my head down and said nothing, hoping the colonel would continue his complaints. He did not.

"I've heard that the rebels have an awful lot of gunpowder." I shook my head. "But it's just a rumor, not worth mentioning."

"Mention it, boy."

"Some say the Patriots just had a big shipment of powder—eighteen hundred barrels worth," I said. "They don't know what to do with it all."

Stockdale glared at me. "Patriots? You mean *rebels*, don't you, boy?"

I stood at attention. Had I just ruined everything with my careless slip of the tongue? "Rebels, sir," I stammered.

He finished his rum without another word and left the tavern, slamming the door behind him. He walked in the direction of the Province House— General Gage's headquarters.

I could only hope he believed me.

A few days later, I had my answer. At the pump Thursday morning the gossip was all about the gunpowder. Only now the rumor had grown. Some said that the rebels had three thousand barrels—enough to wipe out the entire British army.

My buckets full, I shouldered my yoke and walked

toward the tavern. A couple of Redcoats came toward me, laughing so hard they fell into each other. Drunk, I thought, and up all night. Then I saw the object of their laughter.

A company of Loyalists marched down the street, getting ready to drill on the Common. A few such companies had been formed to help defend the town should the rebels attack. The drummer tripped on the cobblestones, sending the Redcoats into new gales of laughter.

The drummer looked up, his face burning with shame and anger. It was Josiah.

The Redcoats rewarded him with more laughter. These men were on the same side as they were, and still the British made sport of them.

Josiah's eyes locked on mine. My presence must have made his humiliation even worse. He pressed his lips together and raised his hands. He had a tight grip on the drumsticks and aimed to throw them at the Redcoats' heads.

I dropped my bucket. The noise it made caught Josiah's attention, and I shook my head no.

Josiah let out a breath and lowered his arms.

He marched on with the militia, his eyes on the cobblestones. A choir of laughing soldiers marched behind him.

CHAPTER SIXTEEN

"Be careful, Prescott, with that war of yours."

August, 1775

The town remained quiet, with no major cannon-ading from either side. Sarah learned to sleep through all but the loudest and longest bursts of fire. Summer gave way to early autumn and took the worst of the heat with it. I dreamed of crisp fall apples and juicy pears, but of course there were none to be had.

I heard that some in town were dining on rats. The sickness continued, but none in our tavern had the pox.

In the middle of September a British supply ship made it to Boston without being captured by the Patriots. It had every kind of provision, and we were immediately more cheerful. I took Sarah to Long Wharf to watch the unloading. All of Boston seemed to be in attendance, cheering as each crate and barrel was unloaded.

Live chickens, sheep, and lambs, and even cows were driven from the ship. Barrels and barrels of good things to eat. Seagulls swooped overhead, searching for bits and pieces of food. A sailor threw a potato at a boy, and he held it as if it were gold.

I remembered a time when all of Boston's wharves were like this. Full of ships loading and unloading. Merchant ships with holds full to bursting. Ships from the West Indies that brought us lemons and pimientos, rum and sugar. Fancy clothes from England. I hoped one day we would see such again. Boston was a grand town then.

I wondered if Father had good things to eat. The farmers in the countryside were treating the soldiers well. I hoped they had enough food.

Sarah ran to the crates of chickens and peered through the slats, searching for Robin Goodfellow and Jacky Juggle. She never made the connection between the missing chickens and the stew pot.

The chickens' cackles sent her into gales of laughter. Her joy at such a simple thing brought happiness to everyone near. A sailor from the ship handed her a carrot, and she immediately tried to feed it to the chickens. When they snapped at it with their beaks she laughed all the more.

Josiah Henshaw sauntered up to us. His drum hung about his neck. "What will you do with that carrot?"

"Feed my chickens," Sarah said.

"Sarah, chickens don't eat carrots," I told her. "But perhaps we can find Star and feed it to her."

"Will you let me use it to bang my drum?" Josiah asked, holding up a drumstick. "I've lost one of my sticks."

Sarah giggled and made a dull bang on his drum with the carrot.

Josiah took it from her and began to beat a lively tune. His playing was better than the last time I saw him. So was his mood. But why had he sought us out?

"Sarah try?" she asked.

Josiah smiled and put the drum around her neck, tying a loose knot in the strap so that the instrument would not hang to her ankles. Together we watched her bang out a tune for the chickens.

"Sing, chickens," she commanded.

We laughed as the chickens commenced to cackle.

"I'm surprised you haven't taken up the drum for one of the Loyalist militias," Josiah said to me. "We're sure to learn of any British plans before the rest of the town."

Was Josiah recruiting drummers and fifers for the Loyalist militias? Was he trying to trick me with talk of British plans? "My work at the tavern keeps me too busy," I said.

He gave me a serious look. "Yes, you have a war of your own, don't you?"

I fought to keep my face expressionless, but I felt my eyes widen with surprise.

"I've never heard of such a war as this one," he continued. "People change sides with each change in the weather. A body has to be very careful when it comes to trusting another—even longtime friends."

Still, I said nothing. I did not understand his meaning, and I feared giving myself away.

"Come, Sarah, I need my drum," Josiah told her. "My soldiers don't march properly without it."

Sarah let him take it from around her neck and held out his drumstick along with the carrot.

"I found my stick!" He pulled the other drumstick out of his pocket. "But I thank you kindly for the use of your carrot." He bowed solemnly and Sarah giggled.

I was not surprised he had his stick all along. He had not joined us for the use of a carrot, but what did he want with this talk of trust?

He turned to me again. "Be careful, Prescott, with that war of yours."

I grabbed Sarah's hand and held it tight. Did Josiah know about my secret activities? Was I in danger? Was Sarah? I hurried home, dragging Sarah as fast as her little legs would go. I looked over my shoulder at every turn expecting soldiers to pounce at any moment. Even home did not bring relief. It was full of the enemy.

Each day and night I waited to be arrested. Nothing happened. Colonel Stockdale and the other officers continued to act in the same manner as they always had toward me. They called me boy and ordered me about and complained when the food was not to their liking. Their demands for rum and ale were no more bad mannered than before.

Whatever Josiah Henshaw thought he knew, I guessed that he had not shared it with the British. In time I relaxed.

A couple of weeks later the *Cerberus* arrived again from London. Colonel Stockdale discussed the news it brought with the officers while they waited for Mother's good dinner. A saddle of mutton—the last of the recent bounty—cooked on the hearth. Our hired soldier manned the tap. I had no reason to be in the dining room until it was time to serve the meal, and so waited behind the door, straining to hear.

I gleaned what I could, and the news was big. General Gage was being recalled to England, and General Howe was to take his place. Stockdale spoke of reinforcements presently on their way to Boston— five or six regiments of regulars at one thousand soldiers each, and one thousand marines. They were expected before winter, and Stockdale was sure Howe would use them to end the rebellion once and for all.

The next morning I set out to find barber Newell. Surely he would want to bring this information to General Washington. If the Patriots were to attack the town, they would have to do so before the reinforcements arrived.

The barber's shop was closed up tight. Had he been arrested? Was he in the Patriot camp? I feared asking his neighbors. If any of them were Loyalists and knew of his secret activities, I would expose myself as a spy. I went back the next morning and again found the same locked door. The same empty house.

If General Washington was to get this news, I would have to bring it to him myself.

CHAPTER SEVENTEEN

Between Two Armies

Two armies stood between me and General Washington. The British and the Patriots. I turned over the ways I might sneak into the Patriot camp while I filled my buckets at the pump. The British had stopped issuing passes to fishing boats on the suspicion that fishermen carried information to the Patriots. I could not ask Colonel Stockdale for a pass. There was no reason for me to go to the country.

Mother was washing the breakfast things when I returned. I added water from one of my buckets to the pot that hung over the fire and set to work helping her.

"Did you see your friend this morning?" she asked.

I shook my head. The back door was open to let in the warm September sunshine. We could not speak freely. "I hoped to post a letter to my friend, but it appears as if I will have to pay a visit instead."

Mother's brow wrinkled with concern. She checked the tavern to make sure it was empty, then closed the back door.

"It is too dangerous, Daniel," she said.

I pretended to be braver than I was. "I have no choice. The barber is not about. I have to get this information to General Washington."

"How will you get there?" she asked.

"I will have to make my own pass and go across the Neck."

She shook her head. "What if you are caught?"

"I will have a pass granting me the freedom to cross the Neck. No one will know it is a forgery." I wanted to sound certain, but my voice quivered.

"This war will be the death of all of us," she said.

My voice was stronger now. "No. It won't be the death of me. Or of Father." I wasn't as sure as I pretended to be. I felt I had no choice, and I didn't want Mother to worry any more than was necessary.

That afternoon luck was with me. All the officers were out. I crept into the colonel's room and used his own quill and ink to write myself a pass. Master Richardson had taught me well. My hand was sure and strong, like an English gentleman's. Inside, I quivered like a frightened baby.

Once again Mother replaced my buttons with coins. She and our hired man would serve the officers while I slipped away. I would not be missed.

It was nearing dark when I took my leave. Mother let me pretend that I shivered from the cold and not from fear. In return, I pretended not to notice the tears in her eyes.

"I'll be back as soon as I can," I whispered, kissing her on the cheek.

"God be with you, Daniel," she said, her voice husky.

I slipped out into the night and made my way to Orange Street and the Neck. The British fortifications were in view. I patted my pocket to make sure the pass was still there.

A guard trained his musket on me as I approached. Two more stood near but made no move toward us.

"Urgent business on behalf of the general," I said, trying to sound like Colonel Stockdale. I waved my pass in the air and kept walking.

"Not so fast." He lowered his musket and took the pass. "Which general?" he asked, scanning the paper.

I realized he could not read.

"Howe," I said, trying to take the pass from him again. My hand trembled like an old woman's.

He held his arm out of my reach and narrowed his eyes. "Why would General Howe send a child into enemy territory on urgent business?"

"Because," I sputtered, "a man would raise too much suspicion."

The other guards edged nearer, alerted by the tone of the soldier's voice. I thought to run, but the pass held Stockdale's signature. If I left it behind, he would surely learn that I had forged it.

"What's the problem, Barker?" one of the soldiers asked.

Barker's attention shifted just for a second. I snatched the pass from his hand and ran as fast as I could.

"Stop!"

"Halt!"

A musket fired, and then another, but I kept running. Something hit my shoulder. A bullet whistled past my ear. I remembered Mother's words. "This war will be the death of all of us," and how I had promised her I would be careful. Now I was going to die like that soldier on the side of the road, alone.

My side ached and my legs felt like they were about to give out. I ran until I couldn't run one step more and threw myself behind a bush. I didn't know if the guards followed. I lay there trembling and tried to gather my wits. I heard them running and tried to quiet my breath, but my lungs could not take in enough air. Could they not hear my loud panting?

My shoulder burned. My fingers found a hole in my jacket but no blood. The bullet had only grazed me. My chest heaved with relief for a moment, but footsteps rustled in the grass quite near. I closed my eyes and strained to hear voices above the night sounds, sure the Redcoats would find me any moment. I fortified myself for the shot that would end my life. Mother had been right. I would die in the war.

A soldier came very near. I lay as still as a statue, and he moved in another direction.

"He's disappeared," one of the soldiers said.

"Just a scared boy anyway," another answered. "There's no harm in him. Let's go."

My body was stiff and sore from laying in one place for so long. My head hurt from listening so hard. I got to my knees and then my feet, looking for Redcoats. But they had truly gone.

My hide was intact, but I felt I had lost all my courage. Even so, it would be more dangerous to try and sneak back into Boston now than to keep going. I broke into a steady run.

Too late, I saw a flash. The next thing I knew, my hat was blown off.

I hit the ground with a cry and clutched the top of my head. Slowly I moved my hands in front of my eyes. I blinked in the darkness. I could hardly believe it, but there was no blood. Footsteps came near, running through the brush.

"It's only a boy!"

I lay with my face in the dirt, afraid to look at them, but their boots were not black and shiny. They were not British.

"Get up, child, and state your business," said another voice.

He pulled on my arm and I stood, shaking.

There were two of them—those wild men Father had warned me about. One had black hair and round, black eyes like the end of a musket. He looked like a devil. The other had lighter hair and was more human.

I opened and closed my mouth like a fish, gulping for air. "I have to see my Father and General Washington," I said in a hoarse whisper. "I come from Boston."

The human one held my cap. "I told you not to shoot," he said to the black-haired devil. "The captain will have your hide."

He shrugged. "I aimed to miss."

"You almost didn't," said the other, sticking his

finger through the hole in my cap. I had come that close to dying.

After a search for weapons I did not have, they asked what my business was with General Washington.

"I have information of British plans," I said.

"What information?" the devil asked.

I feared refusing, but I did not know these men. "I will not tell you. My information is for General Washington."

They snorted with laughter but escorted me to an officer. He laughed as well, but made sure I had a soldier escort. It wasn't until I was near Cambridge that another officer gave me leave to go on alone. I was glad to be rid of them and their snickering.

★ CHAPTER EIGHTEEN ★

A Spy Revealed

I made my way to headquarters as quickly as I could without breaking into a run and giving anyone else cause to shoot me. It felt like days had passed since I had said good-bye to Mother, but the sun was just coming up. I did not warm to the idea of being laughed at again, or shot at again, and so I skirted the town of Cambridge and came up behind the mansion that Dr. Church, the army's surgeon general, claimed as his headquarters.

I spotted Master Richardson peering out of Dr. Church's back door. I was about to call out to him when he signaled to someone. A man I didn't know ran forward and took a sheaf of papers from him before running off again. The schoolmaster slipped back into the house.

I continued on my way, coming to the front of Dr. Church's house just as Master Richardson left by the front door.

"Daniel," he exclaimed, looking alarmed at my appearance. "Where did you come from?"

"I have news for General Washington," I said. "I forged a pass."

His eyes settled on the hole in my jacket and the one in my cap.

I could not say more as there was a commotion in front of Washington's headquarters. A group of officers seemed to be arguing. Dr. Church was at their center, protesting vigorously.

"You find us in an uproar," the schoolmaster told me. "Dr. Church has been discovered writing to the Redcoats in cipher. An army chaplain broke the code. There is no question. Church is a British spy."

I gaped at him. Dr. Church a spy? He was a Son of Liberty. How could he betray a cause he fought for—a cause he believed in? Josiah's words came back to me. *People change sides with each change in the weather. A body has to be very careful when it comes to trusting another.*

"I have just given more coded pages to an aide

to be translated." The schoolmaster eyed me for a reaction, then brought the conversation back to me. "What is this news you have for General Washington?" he asked.

Should I tell him? I looked for Father. He was not on duty in front of headquarters.

"I'd like to talk to my father," I said weakly. "Or the general."

He nodded, but his manner was displeased. "Come," he commanded.

I followed him into the house and stood behind him when he knocked on a door. I recognized Washington's powerful voice. "Enter."

Master Richardson stepped in. Men I took to be officers surrounded the general.

"Sir, I regret to say that someone has already been through his papers," the schoolmaster said. "There is nothing to shed light on any other activities, or to damage him further."

"Thank you, that will be all."

"Ah," Master Richardson moved aside. "You have a visitor."

"Why have you brought me this boy?" General Washington asked. "I am much too busy now."

He did not know me. My shock and fear and relief in my safety all rolled into one and I burst into tears, weeping like a child. I was deeply ashamed, but I could not stop.

"He is Prescott's son—the boy from Boston."

The general's expression softened. He drew me into the room and quickly took charge. "Master Richardson, go and find his father. Sergeant, lay a fire. The boy is cold."

There was a sudden bustle of activity. My sobs settled to whimpers and soon I had control of myself again. Someone handed me a tankard of ale, and I drank it down in gulps.

His Excellency eyed me gravely. He reached forward and took my cap, poking his finger through the musket hole. Then Father rushed into the room and General Washington bid everyone else to leave us.

Father knelt in front of my stool and kissed my forehead, right in front of the general. Normally I would have told him that I was too old for kisses, but in truth I felt better for his having done it.

"Mother and Sarah are fine," I told Father before saying anything else. "Sarah has not gotten the pox—indeed, none in the tavern have gotten the disease."

"That's fine, Daniel," Father said.

I turned to General Washington. Suddenly I was afraid. Would he call me a child, too? Laugh at me? "I have news of the British. General Gage has been recalled to London. Stockdale thinks Howe will attack you as soon as reinforcements arrive—they are on the way to Boston even now."

The General thanked me. Father stood with a sigh.

I had risked my life for this moment, but neither the general nor Father seemed much impressed with my news. "I have brought you coins," I told Father. "My buttons."

He nodded, and it was then that he noticed the bullet hole in my jacket. His eyes got wide, and when he turned to say something to the general he saw the twin hole in my cap, still resting on the general's finger.

"Daniel, why didn't you go to Master Richardson's friend—the barber?" Father asked.

"He wasn't there. Two days he wasn't there," I explained. "I didn't know what to do, so I came myself. I forged a pass. Only the British shot at me, and then the wild men shot my cap off."

"Barber Newell? Is he your contact?" General Washington asked.

I nodded.

"He was here in camp," the general said. "He returns to Boston this morning."

"Daniel, I forbid you to come back to camp," Father told me. "No matter what. If you can't get your information to the barber or to someone else we trust, then the Continental army will have to go on without it. Win or lose."

I expected the general to protest, but he did not.

"Daniel, your father is right. Do you not think I have other spies in Boston? Other ways of getting information?"

I hadn't thought, but of course the general would have many spies.

"You are the second person to bring me this news."

I slumped into the chair. He already knew. Had I risked my life for nothing?

"I am very grateful to have this information confirmed, but it's not worth your young life. Obey your father. You must keep yourself safe." General Washington regarded me seriously. "Promise me, Daniel."

"I promise, sir." The words tasted bitter in my mouth. I thought my work was important. I thought it could mean the difference between liberty and tyranny, between Father's life and Father's death. I had not thought that I was merely one of many. A boy to be chuckled over by wild men while the real spies, like Master Richardson and the barber, did their work.

★ CHAPTER NINETEEN ★

A Curious Rescue

I slept through most of the morning and spent the afternoon in camp with Father. Just before dark, we learned of the general's plan for my return to Boston. The barber had left the morning I arrived, so I needed another guide. I was to be rowed across the water and around north Boston at high tide and under the cover of darkness.

Father made me promise again and again that I would not try to return to camp no matter how important my information. I swore that I would obey. He gave me a letter for Mother, in which he told her the same thing. I wondered when I would see him again. Mayhap he wondered, too. He took me by the shoulders and stared into my face as if to burn it into his memory.

"You are a good boy, Daniel," he said. "I know that Mother and Sarah are safe with you."

Tears welled in my eyes and I pressed my lips together to keep from crying.

He kissed me on the forehead, and I buried my face in his chest for a moment. Then I left with my guide to Boston.

The plan seemed a dangerous one, but I soon learned that the man, whose name I was never told, had often made this very same trip. At water's edge we climbed into a small boat. The oars were wrapped in fabric to muffle their sound, and we pushed off into the water.

I was warned not to speak. Once or twice the man motioned me to duck as we made our silent way across the water. I was grateful for the clouds that hid the moon and the stars, keeping us from British eyes. We came right alongside a British ship. The sound of our oars slipping into the water suddenly seemed as loud as musket fire to my ears. I steeled myself as I listened for shouts, followed by bullets. But none came.

Finally we pulled up right under Hunts Wharf, where the man secured the boat. He put a finger on his lips to signal continued silence as he led me to Lynn Street with a hand on my arm. When we reached the street he turned his head in every direction. Satisfied that no one lurked nearby, he nodded.

"Go straight home," he said.

I took a few steps, and then thought to express my gratitude. But when I turned to whisper my thanks, he was already gone.

I arrived home to another uproar. Our hired man had never arrived the evening before. Mother was only told that he was missing. Many a common soldier had slipped away in the nights since the siege began.

I had left my hat behind in the Patriot camp so that the bullet hole would not trouble Mother, but there was naught I could do about my coat. I was grateful for the busyness of the night. She had no time for questions. As soon as she was assured of my safety and Father's, she handed me clean tankards to carry into the taproom. I didn't even have time to remove my coat.

Mr. Henshaw had dined with the colonel, a rare happening, and stayed to play cards. I was pouring rum for the two of them when Colonel Stockdale's eyes flicked to my missing buttons.

"What have you been up to?" he asked.

I pretended not to understand his meaning. "Searching for a fisherman willing to sell a fresh fish for your dinner tomorrow," I said. "There was none to be had."

He pointed to my chest. "Did you try to pay with buttons?"

Mr. Henshaw chuckled. I glared at him. I had been laughed at enough. "I fought with another boy." I looked over my shoulder and then whispered, "Don't tell Mother, she'll have my hide, sir."

Stockdale said nothing, only examined the hole in the shoulder of my coat—the one made by a British musket ball—and eyed me suspiciously. Then he turned back to Mr. Henshaw and his cards. I was dismissed.

I kept my head down and concentrated on doing my work for the remainder of the night. I forgot all about Stockdale and his mistrust until the next morning.

"Come, boy," he commanded after breakfast. "I have something I wish you to see."

He kept a hand on my shoulder as he led us north on Fish Street. Mother had already replaced my buttons and darned the hole in my coat and I was glad of it. Mayhap the colonel had forgotten about our exchange the night before.

The morning was a warm one, but a chill passed through me as the colonel relayed a story about a barber who had been caught swimming back to Boston from the Patriot camp yesterday. It had to be my barber—Barber Newell. A few hours had kept me from returning to town with him.

"What word have you of your father in *Connecticut?*" the colonel asked.

His emphasis on Connecticut raised alarm bells. He barely suppressed a smirk.

"My grandmother continues in ill health," I stammered. "Father must stay to mind the family business."

"I thought the family business was whaling," the colonel said. "Surely your grandmother doesn't wield a harpoon."

"She . . . she runs a public house," I said.

"I imagine the country in the Connecticut colony looks much like the area around Boston," he said. "I'm sure your father feels like he's barely left Massachusetts."

I could only nod, not trusting my mouth to form words. The colonel's meaning was clear. He knew my father was among the Patriots. My mind darted from one thought to the next. Were Mother and Sarah and I in danger? Did the colonel know of my spying for the Patriots?

Dread came over me as we turned toward Copp's Hill. The colonel aimed to teach me a lesson as surely as he had taught the people of Boston a lesson when he tarred and feathered that peddler last March.

A man sat on top of a horse with his hands tied in front of him and a noose around his neck. The rope was attached to the strong branch of an oak tree. The horse snorted heavily and danced in place, as if it did not want to perform its ghastly duty.

"Behold the barber," the colonel said. He moved his hand to the back of my neck and held me with a tight grip, ensuring that I could not look away.

Had I arrived in General Washington's camp a little sooner, I would be sitting on a second horse. I could almost feel the rope about my neck.

A crowd of soldiers and others jeered at the man. They urged the hangman to hurry, shouting for blood. Mr. Henshaw was one of the loudest. Josiah himself stood next to his father. I hardly recognized him. He was not wearing his customary wig. His blond hair was simply tied in a queue.

My eyes were drawn back to the tree. The hangman must have asked the barber if he had any final words.

"Liberty!" he shouted, just before a feed bag was pulled over his head.

The hangman slapped the horse's rear and it lurched forward, out from under the barber. His legs dangled and the rope tightened around his throat. I hoped his neck would break with a snap and he would die quickly. He did not. The barber's legs danced, searching for purchase.

I tried to twist out of the colonel's grip, but he grasped me tighter.

"Do not look away, boy. This is the fate of traitors and spies. You are old enough to know exactly how such men pay for their treason."

The barber's body jerked like a wooden toy. It sickened me. Then he went still and I sickened even more. My breakfast threatened to come up and cover the colonel's shiny black boots.

I wished it would. I was angry. Angry at the colonel for making me watch such a thing. Angry at the crowd for treating this death like a sport. Angry at the army—at both armies—for bringing us to war.

I wanted to scream and shout, but my throat could only produce a shaky groan. It was Josiah Henshaw who came to my rescue.

"Good show, colonel," he said before turning to me. "Daniel, did your mother have your hide last night over your buttons?"

"What?" I asked, too startled to say more.

"Daniel and I met each other in the street last night and had a game of marbles," he said to the colonel. "I was about to win at ringer when a group of street thugs set upon us and started a fight. Daniel lost his buttons."

His father was at the tavern when I told my story. But was Josiah laying a trap, or giving me a gift? I laughed nervously. "Aye, she was angry, all right," I said. "But don't tell her I was fighting, she'd really have my hide then."

The colonel's grip on the back of my neck loosened, but he said nothing.

Josiah's eyes bore into mine as if we were having one of our old staring matches. I was too startled to join in the sport.

"I have to get back to the tavern," I stammered, backing away from the two of them. "There's much work to do." I started down the hill.

"Daniel?"

I looked back over my shoulder.

Josiah tossed something to me. "You forgot this yesterday."

I reached out and caught it.

"Your lucky shooter," he said.

"Thanks," I croaked, and hurried away.

What was Josiah trying to tell me? I could not ask in front of Colonel Stockdale. For now I only rolled the marble around in my hand, enjoying the way it fit, the perfect weight and size of it. Maybe one day I would play marbles again.

CHAPTER TWENTY

Smallpox

December, 1775

I woke up many a night in mid-gasp, a nightmare image of the barber's dangling feet burned into my brain. I did not understand the meaning behind Josiah's actions that day. Was he a secret Patriot? Or was he setting a trap?

There were rumors of a Patriot assault. For several nights in October and November the entire British army was ordered to sleep in their clothes. Redcoats paraded through the streets all night long, ready to raise an alarm. I wished and prayed that General Washington would indeed attack, but no assault was forthcoming.

The rumored British reinforcements never arrived. I never learned why. General Howe seemed as reluctant as General Gage to attack the Patriot camp. It seemed sure that Boston would spend another winter under British command.

As the cold weather neared, firewood became almost as dear as fresh meat. Much of my time was consumed with the search for wood. I traveled around town picking up anything that would burn. Twice I saw Josiah but ducked into alleys before he could see me. I turned his behavior over and over in my mind, but I couldn't make any sense of it.

The Redcoats had taken to dismantling wharves and old buildings for burning. But they weren't content with destroying our town for wood. The Light Horse Regiment turned Old South Meeting House into a riding school for officers. The very same pulpit that Dr. Warren had stood behind last March was hacked to pieces, along with the pews, for burning. Deacon Hubbard's beautiful carved pew was removed and turned into a pigsty. Then they carted in dirt and hay before leading in their horses. Even Loyalists were outraged by the insult.

November and December brought cold and snow. The early winter was uncommonly severe. The wind was like to cut you in half. Old North Meeting House soon became fuel to keep us from freezing. I often thought of Father and General Washington and wondered if the Patriots fared better than we did.

Then something happened that drove every thought from my mind but one.

On a freezing morning in December, I stood in front of our fire, trying to warm myself. Sarah sat at the table wrapped in a quilt. Suddenly she threw it off and laid her head down.

"Hot," she said. "My head hurts."

I placed a cold hand on her forehead and she flinched. She was burning up with fever.

Mother came downstairs from cleaning the officers' rooms, and we put Sarah to bed with extra quilts and a warm brick at her feet. One minute she shivered, the next she complained of being hot. She could not keep her food down, not even the precious egg that Mother somehow found for her.

We watched and prayed, hoping for the best. But four days later we saw the first sores in her mouth, and soon her whole body was covered in an angry, oozing rash. Smallpox. Mother and I were both safe from the disease, having been inoculated four years ago. The light cases we had then protected us now.

All of our officers had also had the disease, and so could stay in the tavern. We hung a red flag outside to warn others to stay away. We feared Stockdale would force us to send Sarah to the hospital where there were too many patients and few to care for them. The hospital would surely mean death.

Mother was all consumed with caring for Sarah. She gave up waiting on the officers. I did my best to fill in. I served cold, salted meat and paid a boy to gather whatever wood he could. Everything we had was used to keep Sarah warm.

One evening Colonel Stockdale came into the kitchen to complain. I was coming out of Mother and Sarah's bedroom with linen to be boiled. The colonel stuck his head in the room, took one look at Sarah, and turned on his heel. I steeled myself for the order to send Sarah away. Instead, I learned that Colonel Stockdale had a heart.

Two hours later our barn was filled with wood and an army doctor arrived to examine the patient. There was nothing he could do. Sarah was too weak to be bled.

That night I tried to stammer my thanks, but the colonel only waved me off. He never asked after Sarah, but each day found something that might tempt her to eat. An egg, fresh chicken for the stew pot, and even a molasses cake. Sarah only cried when Mother tried to feed it to her.

She was often out of her mind with fever. Mother was the only one who could soothe her. On the rare occasions when Mother left her bedside, Sarah fretted and cried. My efforts to ease her discomfort were useless. I felt as worthless to Sarah as I was to Father and General Washington.

I wondered if Father knew of her illness and prayed he did not. He would try to get back to us if he did. Colonel Stockdale would show no mercy if Father was caught, and I had no wish to see Father's legs dance like the barber's had.

After a fortnight the horrible, oozing rash developed scabs, and we rested easier. Sarah had made it through the worst phase of the sickness. She would live. I was relieved to see that she would have just one pockmark on her pretty little face, on the side of her nose.

On the first day of seventeen hundred and seventy-six I woke to find Mother preparing a breakfast and Sarah sleeping peacefully, with no fever. We were still under siege, but suddenly we had much to be grateful for. My steps were light when I shouldered the yoke and headed for the town pump.

With the new year, the Patriots had raised a new flag on Prospect Hill. As soon as I could, I ran to the top of Beacon Hill to see it for myself. An officer lent me his spyglass, and I watched the banner flap in the icy wind. There were thirteen red and white stripes.

I guessed for the thirteen colonies. In the upper left corner was a small British Union Jack.

"Do they aim to surrender?" asked a Redcoat.

"I think not," said another. "Perhaps they wish to signify the fact that they do not seek independence, like the king said."

"The king?" I asked them, handing back the spyglass.

"King George's speech to parliament. Newly arrived from England," the Redcoat told me. "He said the rebels were trying to start an independent empire."

"Independent empire," I repeated, almost to myself. The colonies had always been a part of England. The Patriots fought for our rights as free Englishmen, not for independence from her.

The soldier mistook my meaning. "We'll crush them," he told me. "We'll crush them if it takes everything we have."

I nodded, but I couldn't wait to get away and ponder the notion further. Why did we need a king across the ocean? What had parliament ever done for us that we could not do for ourselves? "Independence," I said again on my walk down the hill. I liked the way the word felt in my mouth.

"Independence."

★ CHAPTER TWENTY-ONE ★

The Free and Independent States of America

January, 1776

The king's speech was all over town. In it he breathed revenge on the rebels, but promised mercy to those who gave up. There was no mention of restoring our rights. I thought it more likely to stir up talk of independence than to encourage the Patriots to surrender.

Words in support of independence were passed from hand to hand in a pamphlet called *Common Sense* a few weeks later. To Colonel Stockdale, it was simply another thing to mock.

"Common sense," he sneered, throwing the pamphlet into the fire. "The day this rabble is capable of ruling itself, I'll be the first one on a ship sailing for home."

His officers shouted oaths in agreement, but I found my-self silently repeating one of the phrases I heard him read.

The free and independent states of America.

The words moved through me and in me. The notion no longer felt radical, but natural and right. I wished to talk to Father about it. He had often said that King George would come to his senses and restore our rights. But the king had done the opposite. Had Father begun to wish for independence from England instead of peace with her, as I had? Had General Washington?

I would have to wait to find out. In February the winter turned mild. My hopes for a Patriot attack over the ice were crushed—the bay froze one day and thawed the next. I did not understand why Howe did not attack the Patriots himself. Stockdale groaned about it along with his officers. It was said that Howe believed the entire countryside was against the British, and so he remained in Boston. Mayhap he thought the Patriots would tire and go back to their homes. But as long as Boston had to depend on food and all the other necessities of life arriving by English ship, it seemed to me that the Patriots could hold out longer than the British.

Patriot seamen captured many a British supply ship, but one made it through and we were able to avoid starvation for another few weeks. Sarah grew stronger day by day, but I worried what would happen when the food ran out.

It seemed as if nothing would ever change. And then it did. Josiah Henshaw lurked by the town pump early one February morning. There was no escaping him.

"Daniel, can you meet me behind my father's shop on Long Wharf this afternoon?" he asked in a whisper.

I blinked in surprise. "Why?"

"You will not believe me unless you see it with your own eyes," he said. "You must come."

I stood, balancing the yoke over my shoulders. "I can't. I have too much work to do."

"Please," he said, his tone desperate.

Was he laying a trap? "If you will not tell me why, then why should I come?" I pushed past him. Water from my buckets spilled onto the street and his shoes.

He stepped in front of me again. "Remember what I did for you on Copp's Hill?" he asked.

I nodded. Whatever his intentions, I knew I

must be grateful to him for saving me from Colonel Stockdale's suspicions.

"This is an even greater service," he insisted. "You must trust me."

Trust Josiah Henshaw? I almost snorted.

"Please, Daniel," he said again. "You will not be sorry. Upon my word. Upon everything you believe in. You must come."

Finally, I agreed.

"Tell no one," he whispered. "Do not allow yourself to be seen."

I was even more puzzled. "What will happen if I am seen?"

"All will be lost—for us both."

I worried about the meeting all morning long. One minute I decided I would go. The next, I would not. I rolled my lucky shooter in my fingers. I remembered Josiah's boasts on the day he won it, and the great service he had done for me on the day he returned it. Finally, I decided I would do as he asked—but carefully—ready to run at the first sign of a trap.

I told Mother that there were rumors of fresh fish for sale on Long Wharf, and she gave me permission to go. I kissed a napping Sarah good-bye and left.

I kept to the alleys as best I could, passing only

Redcoats on my way. Josiah's father's shop was shuttered in the middle of the day, an odd occurrence. Josiah was huddled behind the building. He pulled me to him with a signal to be quiet.

There was a noise from within. Josiah motioned to me to peer around the corner.

Master Richardson was leaving the shop with Mr. Henshaw and two British officers! They were laughing.

Josiah pulled me back just as Master Richardson turned. Had he seen me?

"Make it look good, gentleman," the schoolmaster said. "There may be eyes about."

The officers each took one of the schoolmaster's arms as if he was a prisoner. Was he one? Why was he acting so friendly with the enemy?

"Come. Let us see what Colonel Stockdale thinks of our plan," Mr. Henshaw said.

"And how much he's willing to pay for it," Master Richardson added.

One of the officers nodded. "You'll get your gold. Don't worry."

The small group marched forward, my schoolmaster between the officers.

I turned to Josiah for an explanation. I was too thunderstruck to voice my questions.

"Master Richardson meets with my father whenever he can."

"Is your father a secret Son of Liberty?" I asked.
"No."

All the breath left my body and I had to hold on to the building for support. If Mr. Henshaw was not on the Patriots' side, then my schoolmaster was a traitor. I remembered the morning Dr. Church was exposed as a spy—how I had seen the schoolmaster slip out of Church's back door. Was Master Richardson the reason that Stockdale seemed to know I had visited the Patriot camp? Suddenly it all made sense. But why did Josiah Henshaw reveal this to me?

Josiah read the question in my eyes. "I am the secret Son of Liberty in my family."

"How?" I sputtered. "Why?"

"My father shrugs off their insults," Josiah said. "He expects the British to win this war and everything to go back to the way it was. He cares only about money. I want more than money. I want liberty."

I gaped at him. Was this truly Josiah Henshaw speaking?

"If the British leave Boston, we'll leave with them," he told me. "But Massachusetts is my country. I will find a way to come back."

"How long has Master Richardson been a British spy?" I asked.

"He's been feeding us secrets almost since the war

began—in exchange for money," Josiah said. "Father recruited him. I helped."

I was astonished. Master Richardson had been betraying us for months!

"Master Richardson brags of his position with General Washington. The Patriots must be warned," Josiah urged.

"What is this plan they speak of?"

"I don't know," Josiah said.

"I must get back to the tavern before they do," I said.

Josiah agreed. "Hurry. I'll try to delay them."

We both began to run, staying well behind the group until they turned onto Merchants Row. There was no time for thanks. No time for good-bye. I took to the alleys. Josiah stayed behind the men.

They were just turning onto Fish Street when I got to the tavern. I saw Josiah approach them but could not stop to watch. Mayhap I was about to leap into a trap, but I had no choice. If Master Richardson was truly a British spy, I must find him out.

★ CHAPTER TWENTY-TWO ★

A Stew of Lies

I slipped into the front door and peered around. Stockdale was in the taproom, reading the *Boston News-Letter*, a Loyalist newspaper, and drinking a tankard, as was his mid-afternoon habit. He would not discuss a secret plan in so public a place but would bring the men upstairs. If I could get to the attic above his room, I might be able to hear them.

My heart pounded like a hundred pairs of boots stomping up the stairs, but my footsteps were silent as I made my way into the attic.

I crept to the chimney flue and prayed their voices would reach my ears. I smelled dust and mice, and pinched my nose so as not to sneeze.

I heard muffled sounds from below and then boots on the stairs. Moments later, Stockdale strode in, followed by the others.

I heard the schoolmaster's voice first. "It's all here in my report," he said, handing the papers to the colonel. "Troop levels, artillery positions."

"The rebel army—if you can call it that—is in bad shape," Mr. Henshaw said next. "They're as tired of this siege as we are. They want to go home. Many are deserting."

"We have a plan to end this thing once and for all," Master Richardson added.

Colonel Stockdale was silent for some few minutes. I guessed he was reading the report. Then I heard his booming voice. "What of General Washington?" he asked. "Is he tired, too? Does he want to go home?"

"Washington is a fine military man," the schoolmaster said. "But finer than the men he commands."

I heard Colonel Stockdale snort in disgust.

Master Richardson's voice was oily and smug. "One strong blow will send his soldiers scurrying home," he said.

Someone pounded on the desk, and then I heard Stockdale's angry voice again. "Howe will not attack. I've urged him and urged him. He will not move. In the meantime we sit and rot in this horrible town."

I had to strain to hear Mr. Henshaw's question. "What if you could do more than urge him?"

"Your meaning?"

"What if the Patriots attack Boston?" Master Richardson said next.

Stockdale laughed. "We would crush them. Surely your General Washington knows that would be suicide."

"Washington wants to attack Boston," Master Richardson told him. "If he believes the British plan a major assault, he will convince his war council to strike first. Your counterattack will destroy the entire rebel army in one blow."

"And you believe you can make this happen?" Stockdale asked.

"If I have proper evidence of a British plan—and money enough to risk my hide—I can force Washington's hand," Master Richardson said.

My own hands were in fists. I wanted to fall through the chimney and give the schoolmaster a pounding. How easily he talked of lying to General Washington. Of the destruction of the entire Patriot army. For money!

"Washington will attack Boston, and Howe will be forced to counterattack," Mr. Henshaw added. "You'll be riding across the countryside by the end of the week. The rebels who don't run away with their tails between their legs will be hanging from the gallows."

I listened to them cook up a stew of lies, making sure it was well spiced.

Master Richardson was promised a large sum if the plan worked, and a position with Mr. Henshaw after the war. He was to spend the night at Mr. Henshaw's and "escape" to the rebel camp the next morning with documents that would support his evil deception.

Finally it sounded as if they were preparing to leave. Then I heard my former schoolmaster ask the colonel one last question.

"What about the Prescott boy?"

"I took him to see your barber hang," the colonel said. "He won't be carrying any more information to his father, not if he values his neck."

"I thought I saw him on Long Wharf."

Every one of my muscles tensed. Stockdale answered as they left the room.

"Shoot him if you must."

CHAPTER TWENTY-THREE

"Shoot him if you must."

S*hoot him if you must.*"
The words crashed in my ears. Then I began to think. If the schoolmaster got back to camp and convinced General Washington of his lies, there would be no free and independent states of America. I had to reach Father and General Washington first. But if I was caught, I would surely die.

I had sworn an oath not to return to the camp, but there was no one in Boston I could trust. I decided I would have to break my vow and go myself. I tried not to remember how close I had come to death the last time I made that journey.

I listened as Colonel Stockdale and the others

clumped down the stairs. All who saw them would believe the schoolmaster's terrible trick. Some may even take pity on Master Richardson for being a prisoner. Only I knew that soon he would be in General Howe's office, making a plan to betray us.

Master Richardson had said he would return to the Patriot's camp in the morning. I had to get there tonight, before he "escaped" to carry out his treachery.

I waited until all was quiet below, then left the attic and crept into Stockdale's room. Master Richardson's report lay on top of Colonel Stockdale's table. I slipped it into my waistcoat. A sudden image of the barber's dangling feet flooded my eyes as vividly as if he were right in front of me. Which death would be more painful—hanging or shooting?

I could not think about that now. Instead I took a shaky breath, crept down the stairs, and walked through the taproom into the kitchen. Mother was preparing the evening meal.

"Was your mission a success?" she asked.

I froze. "My mission?"

"Fish, Daniel," she said. "Did you not go out for fish?"

"Oh, ah, yes . . ." I stammered. "There was none to be had."

Suddenly her eyes were sharp, searching my face for signs of danger. "Did something happen?"

"No," I said. "Nothing."

She turned back to the meal. "Master Richardson has been taken prisoner," she said quietly.

I pretended to be surprised. "Oh?"

My reaction was not convincing. Mother's eyes were on my face again. "We must remember him in our prayers."

"Colonel Stockdale wants me to run these papers to General Howe." I pointed to the bulge in my waistcoat and did not meet her gaze.

"Hurry then," she said. "Supper's almost ready and we'll soon have a crowd of soldiers yelling for drink."

Her voice was thick. Did she know what I was about to do? I hated myself for the worry I would cause her, but I could see no other way.

A strand of my hair had slipped from its queue. She gently pushed it behind my ear before running her hand down my cheek and chucking me under my chin. "It looks like it might storm."

I could only nod, not trusting myself to speak. I checked in on Sarah. She slept peacefully. I took *Robin Good-Fellow: A Fairy Tale* and slipped it under her pillow. If I did not return, I wanted her to think that I was helping people and having adventures like Robin. She was the best of sisters, and I did not want to cause her any pain.

I had no plan for making my way to Cambridge.

Trying to cross the Neck without a pass would be impossible. The only other way across was by water. I remembered the boat under Hunt's Wharf and ran there quickly, but it was gone. I would have to make my way on foot.

It was just coming on dark. I kept to the alleys as best I could and skirted around Mill Pond. As mother had said, it soon began to storm. I shivered as rain turned to sleet and back to rain again.

At the tip of Barton Point, I strained to see across the Charles River. The dark and the clouds hid it from me, but I knew Lechmere's Point was across the water. And from there, I could make my way to Cambridge.

I clutched the papers, wrapped in a piece of leather and hidden in my waistcoat, and carefully stepped onto the ice. I took a few careful steps.

Crack!

I slipped and hit the ice. Was that a shot?

Crack!

The noise split the night again. It was not a British musket. It was the ice cracking beneath me. I was close to British fortifications. Could they hear it, too?

The waters were low. If the ice broke I could walk across, but would I survive in the freezing water, even if it was only up to my knees? Or would I freeze to death before I reached the opposite shore?

I tried to tell myself that it had been a misunderstanding. Master Richardson was only playing with the British on General Washington's behalf. It was foolishness to risk my life for something the general already knew—indeed must have planned himself.

Yes. Foolishness. General Washington and the others would only laugh at me. A foolish boy carrying foolish tales. Father would be furious at me for disobeying him and shamed by my claims against the schoolmaster. Tears mixed with rain on my face.

I turned and started back toward the Boston shore. I would go home to Mother and Sarah. Slip the colonel's papers back into his room. If I was quick enough, he would never know they were missing. My steps were halting.

I remembered the time I had seen the schoolmaster leave Dr. Church's headquarters, and how angry he had been when I let Father know that he had worked for Mr. Henshaw. Josiah's words—*Father recruited him. I helped*—came to me again.

Master Richardson was indeed a traitor, and I was likely the only Patriot besides Josiah who knew. I had to risk my cowardly hide to expose him.

I turned around again and stepped across the ice. I was almost to the opposite shore when I broke through. Pain shot up my legs as I sunk partway into the freezing water. I could not feel my toes. My teeth chattered so loudly, I was sure I would give myself away. I clutched at my papers. At least they were dry.

I peered around me. I saw no soldiers on either shore. I slowly put one foot in front of the other, making my way across the icy bay. In time, I was able to walk on ice again. Each time it cracked, I ducked and froze and prayed.

Finally I was across. I had no more to fear from British muskets, but what about those of General Washington's soldiers? Those wild men shot first and asked questions second. I crept up the muddy bank and stayed low, then stopped to take off my shoes and stockings and try to warm the life back into my feet. My toes felt as if they would break off like icicles. My frozen legs and feet were wooden and did not want to move.

The longer I sat on the bank the colder I got. I stood and hobbled forward. A twig broke with a snap and I slipped, falling backward into the mud. I rolled over and crouched in the grass, shaking, sure that I was about to be shot. I waited for the blow, but it didn't come. At last I was able to breathe. I crawled for a few yards before getting to my feet again.

I wanted to run. I wanted to howl. Master Richardson was my friend. I trusted him, and he had turned out to be my enemy. But I could do none of those things. I checked to make sure I still had the papers and forced myself to walk slowly. Finally the Patriot sentries came into view. I told them who I was, and that I had to see the general.

They did not seek out Father, but headed straight for General Washington's headquarters. I pushed my way past the aide who tried to question me and followed the sound of the general's voice.

I stood at the entrance to the dining room. The general sat at the table with a number of men. I recognized some of the military officers. Fine men in fine uniforms. I thought only then of the picture I must have made—wet and frozen and muddy, dripping on the carpet.

"Daniel Prescott! What is the meaning of this?" The general's eyes flashed. His anger was a fearsome thing to behold.

I was too cold and miserable to take notice of the fact that General Washington remembered my name. I shivered so hard I could barely speak. "I have evidence of a traitor," I said, holding my papers. "And a plot to end the rebellion."

★ CHAPTER TWENTY-FOUR ★

Laying a Trap

Some minutes later, I was wrapped in a blanket with my feet in a tub of warm water. Shivering in front of the fire in the general's office, I told the men everything that had happened. I began with the moment Josiah Henshaw approached me at the town pump, and ended with the sure fact that Master Richardson was a traitor.

The Henshaw name raised many questions among the men present. Mr. Henshaw was a well-known supporter of the king.

"Let's hear the boy out," Washington said.

I told them I had seen the schoolmaster hand

papers to someone behind Dr. Church's house in September, and of Stockdale's words this afternoon: "Shoot him if you must."

Each one of their faces held a look of distrust.

"The boy's been misled—or he's lying," General Lee said. "Richardson's been with us since the beginning."

"Is it possible you've been tricked, Daniel?" General Washington asked me.

"Did you send Master Richardson to Boston with this plan?" I asked.

The general shook his head.

"Then no, I have not been tricked."

Someone suggested that the schoolmaster's room be searched. General Lee went with an aide and two other gentlemen.

I was left alone with a guard. A soldier brought me hot soup and a piece of bread, but I could not eat it. What if they found nothing in the schoolmaster's room that would point to his secret activities? What would happen to me?

Father burst into the room. "Daniel!" His face was stern, angry. He was under guard.

Like me, he was now suspected of working for the enemy. My actions had put both of us in danger. The British hanged spies. What did the Patriots do?

I let the tears fall freely while I told Father what had happened to me that day, and how much I wished it not to be true. "But the schoolmaster betrayed us," I choked out. "Who could I trust? I had to come myself."

He sighed and put a hand on my knee to comfort me. "The truth will come out, Daniel. It always does."

A few minutes later, General Washington came back into his office with a sheaf of papers and a codebook. He was angry again, his voice clipped as he ordered the guards to leave us.

"Daniel's story is true," he said. "Mr. Richardson is in league with the enemy."

Father's anger at me had blown away as quickly as the storm. "My son would not make up such a thing."

The other officers joined us and soon they devised a trap. The general warned everyone in the room to tell no one of the schoolmaster's treachery so that he would not be tipped off on his way to camp.

"We'll find a way to use this to our advantage," he said. "The British think this trap will destroy us. Let's turn the tables on them."

I was hobbling out of the room when Father swooped me up into his arms. It was a relief not to have to stand on my feet, but I felt like a child again.

Even so, Old Put patted me on the shoulder as we passed by. "Well done, boy," he said. "Well done."

I shared Father's quarters that night. Neither of us could sleep with the worry over what would happen next.

"What will happen to Mother and Sarah?" I asked. "Surely Colonel Stockdale will figure out that I exposed the schoolmaster."

"The Redcoats have not yet punished the families of Patriots," Father said. "From what you have told me, Colonel Stockdale has done much to see Sarah through the pox. Mother and Sarah are safe."

I remembered that young Paul Revere, the son of the famous silversmith and Son of Liberty, remained in Boston all these months to protect the family's home. The British had not harmed him. They would surely not harm Mother and Sarah. It was my last thought before drifting off to sleep, snuggled against Father for warmth.

By the next morning I could walk again. I was just coming back from the necessary when Master Richardson rushed up the King's Highway, his clothes disheveled. I ducked behind a bush so he would not see me.

He presented himself at headquarters and was immediately taken to General Washington. I slipped into a small chamber next to the office and opened the door a crack so I could see and hear the proceedings. Father stood guard outside.

General Washington sat behind his desk, preparing the General Orders for the day. Old Put stood by the window, and General Lee sat calmly in the corner reading papers that had been found in the schoolmaster's room. He regarded the schoolmaster curiously and then went back to his task.

Master Richardson prattled on with much self-importance about sneaking across the Neck to get a fix on Redcoat positions. Then he babbled about his arrest and his escape. " . . . only just able to get away with my life," he said breathlessly. "But I have certain intelligence about a plan to break across the Neck and crush us entirely. We must attack first."

General Washington eyed him sternly. "Very interesting," he said calmly. "And when is this attack to take place?"

"As soon as Howe's reinforcements arrive," Master Richardson answered. "Troops are on their way from Halifax even as we speak."

Washington nodded, then turned to Old Put. "What say you, general?"

"I say we string him up by the neck."

Master Richardson stiffened.

"We know, sir, what you have been up to," Washington said.

"What . . . what . . . do you mean?" the schoolmaster stammered.

I stepped into the room.

He jumped like a startled deer when he saw me.

"I heard everything," I said. "I was hiding in the attic above Colonel Stockdale's room."

He looked as thunderstruck as I had been the day before. Then his expression hardened into a sneer.

"We know of your treachery," General Lee told him, waving the papers, "thanks to the bravery of this boy."

"Bravery?" Master Richardson repeated with a laugh. "No doubt the boy is lying to save his own skin. I can tell you of his cowardice, but I have never seen bravery in him."

"He brought us this," General Lee said, handing him the report he had given to Stockdale. "Is this not your hand?"

The schoolmaster took the papers from him. "I taught hundreds at the writing school. That could be my hand, or any of my students. No doubt Daniel created this to throw us off his spying activities—or his father's."

"These papers were found in your room," Old Put said. "And this codebook."

Master Richardson shrugged. "Planted there by Daniel or his father."

General Washington's face was stern and angry. I could tell he did not believe the traitor.

Old Put yelled, "Tarnation, man, what were you thinking?"

Master Richardson's eyes landed on me again. "Thank goodness I'm back in time to stop whatever plan this creature has in mind. You know he and his father feed and house the enemy in Boston, do you not?"

General Washington's eyes were on fire. He banged his desk. "Do not cast blame on this brave boy!"

"Brave again? Tell them how brave you were last March the sixth," the schoolmaster sneered. "I saved you—and Dr. Warren and Samuel Adams that day. And you were very happy to accept the tributes for my behavior then, Daniel Prescott. I cannot even guess at what your plan is now."

He looked around the room, seeking support.

The schoolmaster turned to me again. "I assure you, Daniel, you will fail in this evil deed. As surely as you failed the wounded after the battle on Bunker's Hill."

"No one will believe your slander. This boy and his father are loyal Patriots," General Lee told him. "I don't know what you are."

"Some of what he says is true," I told General Washington. I did not meet his eyes. I was too ashamed. "I was a coward. I did not trip the ensign that day in Boston. Master Richardson pushed me into him."

I remembered the soldier who had slumped into me, seeking comfort as he crossed into death. "After the battle . . . I got scared . . . so much blood . . ." My voice trailed off. Would my cowardice ruin my chance to expose the schoolmaster? I couldn't let it. "I ran away then, but everything I said last night is true," I said in the strongest voice I could muster. "Master Richardson has been selling our secrets to the British. He was in league with Dr. Church, and he continued to betray us on his own."

I turned to my former schoolmaster. His eyes bore into mine. They were angry and hateful. I held his gaze steady. "Tyranny must be opposed—that's what you taught me. I don't understand why you've changed," I said. "I thought you were a true Patriot."

Master Richardson blinked and turned away.

"Greed," Old Put roared. "It was simple greed."

"Greed? Greed, you call it?" the schoolmaster snapped. "I call it survival. I was starving in Boston, and you would have let me. At least the British paid me. I would have died a slave to you and your cause."

The questioning went on for another half an hour, then the talk turned to punishment. I slipped outside. I had no stomach for their words about hanging. A short time later, Father and I watched three soldiers escort the schoolmaster to the guardhouse.

How I wished I could be home with Mother and Sarah. But I would not be able to go back to Boston. Colonel Stockdale would surely see me shot or hanged.

CHAPTER TWENTY-FIVE

The Redcoats Set Sail

March, 1776

Father and General Washington agreed that I had better stay in camp. The general assured me that he could get news of my safety to Mother. I did not ask how, nor did he tell me.

The next day, Washington praised me in his daily orders to the troops. He thanked me "for gallant and soldier-like behavior in exposing a traitor in our midst." I tried not to appear boastful when the soldiers patted me on the back and cheered for me, but the general's words lit a fire inside of me. I could not stop grinning.

Father continued his guard duties. I helped where I could, acting as a messenger for the general. The war council met to decide on a plan of action. They decided to draw the British out of Boston, as they had on Bunker's Hill. This time, they'd take the even higher and steeper hills to the south—Dorchester Heights.

Although spring was again in the air, the ground was too frozen to build fortifications in one night. The engineers devised a brilliant plan. We were to build wooden forts in camp and carry them to the top of Dorchester Heights in the dead of night.

The soldiers were pleased to have work to do after so many months of waiting. All about me I heard cutting and hammering. Straw and twigs were twisted into tight bundles to fill the wooden frames. In anticipation of the major battle to come, nurses were called in from the countryside, and nearby citizens were asked to make bandages.

One day I was working on some correspondence for the general when I stopped to admire the plans for the fortifications. I remembered how the Patriots had lost the battle at Bunker's Hill only because they ran out of ammunition. What if there was a way to start winning the battle before the enemy could even advance up the hill?

I dropped my lucky shooter in front of the plans and let it roll off the table.

General Washington looked up from his papers.

"Too bad we don't have giant marbles to roll down the hill," I said.

The general picked up my marble and rolled it off the table as I had. "Barrels would do," he said thoughtfully. "Filled with dirt and rocks." He rolled the marble off the table again and his eyes lit up. "That's a fine idea. They'll fall head over heels."

On the evening of March the second, General Washington ordered a bombardment of Boston from the Patriot lines that were farthest from Dorchester. The British returned fire. At nightfall the next day, we once again began to fire our cannons. I wondered if Stockdale thought his trick had worked. The British commanders must surely be wondering if an attack was forthcoming.

On the third night our cannons thundered again, but the difference was this—the roar of cannon fire blocked the sound of three thousand soldiers marching to the top of Dorchester Heights. Oxen huffed and wagons groaned with the weight of all they carried up the steep slopes, but the British heard none of it. A full moon guided our way, and Washington moved silently on his horse. His strong presence urged the men to hurry in their work.

The dirt and rocks we dug to put the forts in place were used to fill wooden barrels. They were placed in front of the forts, ready to roll at the first sign of an advance.

I could only imagine the reaction in Boston at dawn. The British woke up to discover that six forts now covered the hills, with cannons aimed directly at the town and at the ships in the harbor. Their big guns shrieked, but the cannon shot simply hit the hill. Our men were safe.

Washington's soldiers were ready, even eager for a battle. They were confident they had amassed enough powder to stand against the Redcoats. General Washington gave a stirring speech to the Patriots, reminding them that it was March the fifth—the sixth anniversary of the Boston Massacre. A full year had passed since Dr. Warren gave his speech at Old South.

My plan was to run back to Cambridge when the Redcoats advanced. I had no wish to find myself in the middle of another battle. I wondered at the brave men around me and asked Father about it.

"Only the foolhardy are unafraid, Daniel," he said. "That's not what bravery is. True courage is moving forward when you're most afraid."

"These men are afraid, too?" I asked.

"These men are afraid. But they're willing to persevere because of the strength of our cause," Father said.

The general happened upon us. "Perseverance and spirit have done wonders in all ages," he said. "They're far more powerful than even the mightiest of armies."

I pondered their words as I watched the men around me. Father and the general were right. The Patriot soldiers were not fearless, but steadfast. They believed in the cause. That's where their strength lay—not in fearlessness. No matter what happened in this battle, the Continental army would live to fight on. We would be free of tyranny one day.

We waited for the British to attack. Storm clouds commenced to gather, and then filled the sky. The wind picked up with a howl. What followed was a storm unlike any other I had ever seen. Rain was so thick one could hardly see. The warships along the coast were tossed about like toys.

The Redcoats retreated from the attack position. Our soldiers cheered despite the fearsome weather. The next day, General Howe sent word through the town Selectmen that if he and his troops were allowed to leave Boston unharmed, he would not destroy the town. The storm and the prospect of another battle like the one at Bunker's Hill had defeated the Redcoats.

Our soldiers' celebration at the news was hushed. No one trusted the British to keep their word. We were on alert for attack at all times.

Over the next two weeks, we watched the British and Loyalists scurry about Boston, getting ready to leave. I thought often of Josiah Henshaw, certain that I would find his house empty when I returned. Mr. Henshaw would leave with the British and take his son with him. I hoped that Josiah would find his way back to Boston one day, as he had promised. Without his warning I never would have suspected the schoolmaster, and the British might have been able to crush the Patriot army.

I took a good, long look at Boston through General Washington's spyglass. Much had changed since the siege began. Wharves and buildings were gone—burned for firewood. Many of our citizens had moved to the country, and more would leave with the British. But Boston was still a glorious town, and I was certain it would prosper once again.

One Sabbath morning we watched the troops embark and the warships leave Boston's wharves. I did not stay in camp for the celebration. I hugged Father good-bye. He would stay with his company and await orders but expected to be home—at least for a visit—very soon.

I headed toward the Neck. When I finally reached

Boston, I ran down Orange Street toward Fish Street and home.

Our tavern sign—the blue whale—rocked in the breeze as if to greet me. Mother and Sarah were in the doorway. I threw myself into Mother's arms. Sarah bounced up and down beside me.

"I've missed you, my brave man," Mother said through her tears. Man, not boy.

I hugged her tighter. Perhaps I *was* a man now. A free man.

Boston was free!

★ HISTORICAL NOTE ★

Daniel Prescott and his family are fictional characters, set in a real historical framework. You might be wondering how much of his story is fiction and how much is fact.

In this novel the generals I've named on both sides of the conflict were actual people. Political figures mentioned on both sides were also actual people. Most of the remaining characters, including Lieutenant Colonel Stockdale, are fictional. There were many British officers like Colonel Stockdale in Boston during the siege.

The Siege of Boston lasted for close to a year. The New England militias followed the British back to Boston after the Battle of Lexington and Concord on April 19, 1775, and trapped them in the town. Almost a year later, a "hurrycane" did indeed prevent the British from attacking the Patriots on Dorchester Heights, bringing an end to the siege. On March 17, 1776, 120 British ships sailed from Boston bound for Halifax, Canada, with more than eleven thousand soldiers and Loyalists packed on board.

Except for the Battle of Bunker's Hill (which really took place on Breed's Hill), there were no big military battles during the Siege of Boston. The siege gave the colonial militias time to come together and form an army. By the end of the siege, the Continental Congress in Philadelphia assumed command of the army, and most of the thirteen colonies sent men in support.

Sometimes, even in historical accounts, it's hard to know what's really true. Stories get passed from person to person, and by the time they're written down the facts are fuzzy. Small things can be blown out of proportion. The story of the ensign and the egg is one such anecdote. I read about this plan in a book about Paul Revere—a British ensign was assigned to bring an egg to Old South Meeting House on March 6, 1775, in order to start a riot, but he tripped and fell on his way to the meeting.

No one really knows why the British thought throwing an egg at Dr. Warren would be a good signal to use, or how the ensign fell, but I decided it would be fun to give Daniel the job of tripping the ensign and breaking the egg.

There is no evidence that the British poked fun at the Loyalist militia companies in Boston the way they do in the pages of this novel. It is clear that the Redcoats held the Patriot army in low esteem, and later in the war George Washington decided that the fastest way to turn a Loyalist into a Patriot was to send them back to the British. So, while the scene in which Daniel stops Josiah from throwing his drumstick at a Redcoat is not based in fact, I believe it points to a greater truth.

Other events in the book, like the Battle of Lexington and Concord, the beginning of the siege, and the Battle of Bunker's Hill, are well documented in history books. A group of farmers, fishermen, blacksmiths, and hunters was able to keep the mightiest fighting force on earth trapped in Boston for nearly a year.

Dr. Benjamin Church, a prominent Son of Liberty and the Chief Physician of the Hospital of the Army, did turn out to be a British spy. There were many Patriots and Loyalists who slipped across the lines to bring secrets back and forth. Most of their names are lost to history, but it is likely that more than one boy played a role in these spy networks.

Four months after the British left Boston, a copy of a document from the Continental Congress in Philadelphia made its way to the town. It had been sent to King George in England and declared that the people of the thirteen United States of America had the right to life, liberty, and the pursuit of happiness. This Declaration of Independence was read to cheering crowds from the balcony of Boston's State House on July 18, 1776.

Washington marched his army to New York City shortly after the British retreated from Boston. He left behind a small defense force, but the town never saw military action again during the remaining seven years of the American Revolution. Daniel's father, had he been real and not a fictional character, probably would have been part of that defense force. I like to think that Daniel would have had his father at home with him, or nearby, for the remainder of the war.

CHILDREN'S ROLES *in the*
★ AMERICAN REVOLUTION ★

The youngest person in the Patriot camp around Boston was probably ten-year-old Israel Trask. At the outbreak of the war he left his Marblehead, Massachusetts, home with his father to work in the camp as a messenger and cook's helper.

Boys had to be sixteen to become soldiers, but younger boys often went to war with their fathers to play drums and fifes. Some boys lied about their ages so that they could pick up guns and take their places beside the soldiers. The Continental army, hungry for fighting men, signed them up without asking too many questions.

Girls helped their mothers take care of wounded soldiers, and washed and mended uniforms for the army when it passed through their towns and their farms. Patriot children collected lead, which was needed to make bullets. Families stopped eating lamb because sheep's wool was needed to make soldiers' uniforms.

One Philadelphia family were ingenious secret agents for the Patriots. The Darraghs spied on British officers living in their home. Lydia Darragh wrote down what they learned in code on tiny pieces of paper. Then she put the messages inside her son John's cloth-covered buttons. Fourteen-year-old John regularly slipped across the British lines and gave his buttons to his brother Charles, a lieutenant with Washington's army.

The children living in the colonies at the beginning of the war for independence were ordinary children living in extraordinary times. No doubt there were many young spies and soldiers who didn't make it into the history books. Young people then, like now, were often at the center of events that shaped America.

★ HISTORIC CHARACTERS ★

Some of the characters in Daniel at the Siege of Boston, 1776, *were real people who played a part in the* American Revolution.

THE BRITISH

Major General John Burgoyne, known as "Gentleman Johnny," was a leader of the British garrison during the Siege of Boston. He dismissed the Patriot army as a "preposterous parade." But in 1777, Burgoyne was forced to surrender his own army of 6,000 British troops to those "preposterous" Americans when he was defeated at the Second Battle of Saratoga.

General Thomas Gage fought with George Washington in the French and Indian War. After the Boston Tea Party, King George III named Gage military governor of Massachusetts and sent him to Boston to squash the rebellion. He failed and was replaced as British military commander by General William Howe in October 1775.

George III became the King of Great Britain and the American colonies in 1760. The rebellion in the colonies enraged him, and his opinion of the troops around Boston was not very high.

General William Howe was sent to Boston to support General Gage during the siege. He was in command at the Battle of Bunker's Hill and replaced Gage as commander in chief of British forces in America in October 1775. He, too, failed to squash the rebellion and was replaced by another general before the end of the war.

THE AMERICANS

Samuel Adams of Boston was one of the most radical of the Sons of Liberty. He was a mastermind of the Boston Tea Party, a member of Congress, and an early supporter of breaking ties with England.

Benjamin Church was a prominent member of the Sons of Liberty until Steptember 1775, when he was caught spying for the British. George Washington wanted Church to be hanged for his treachery. Instead, Church was sent into exile on a ship bound for the West Indies. He disappeared at sea.

John Hancock was the richest man in Boston, a prominent Patriot and one of the Sons of Liberty. As chairman of the Continental Congress, he was the first person to sign the Declaration of Independence.

Samuel Langdon was a patriot, pastor, and president of Harvard University in Boston. On June 16, 1775, he led the Patriot soldiers in a "fervent and impressive" prayer before the Battle of Bunker's Hill.

Charles Lee, a retired British officer living in Virginia, supported the American cause and served in the Patriot army. At the time of the siege, he was George Washington's second in command.

Thomas Paine was an English inventor and philosopher with radical notions about liberty. He came to America and in 1776 wrote "Common Sense," a bestseller urging the colonies to declare independence from Britain.

Colonel William Prescott marched his Minutemen from Groton, Massachusetts, to Lexington to meet the British in April 1775. His men then joined the Patriot army encamped around Boston. Along with Colonel Putnam, he was in command at Bunker's Hill.

Israel Putnam, or "Old Put," was a colonel in the Connecticut militia when the fighting started at Lexington. He immediately headed to Boston to take part in the siege and with Colonel Prescott was in command of the Patriots at the Battle of Bunker's Hill.

Paul Revere was a Boston silversmith who became active in the Sons of Liberty. His engraving of the Boston Massacre was well known throughout the colonies. Revere is now most famous for his 1775 "midnight ride" to Lexington to warn the Patriots that the British were coming.

Artemas Ward, veteran of the French and Indian wars, was a Massachusetts farmer and storekeeper. He commanded the Patriot's army around Boston until George Washington arrived. Ward led the parade of American troops into Boston when the siege ended.

Joseph Warren was a Boston doctor and Son of Liberty. At Bunker's Hill he helped many Patriot soldiers to retreat before he was killed. Samuel Adam's grandson wrote of Warren's death: "When he fell, liberty wept."

George Washington was a Virginia planter and hero of the French and Indian War. In 1775 he was unanimously chosen by the Continental Congress to be the commander in chief of the Continental army. He later became the first President of the United States.

★ TIMELINE ★

The Siege of Boston and the American Revolution

1764

April 5   **Sugar Act**   The British Parliament passes the Sugar Act, taxing imports like sugar, coffee, and wine. The thirteen colonies protest.

1765

March 22   **Stamp Act**   Parliament passes the Stamp Act, taxing all printed material, including newspapers. Colonists refuse to buy British goods. Protest riots erupt in Boston

1766

March 17   **Stamp Act Repealed**   A boycott of British goods forces parliament to repeal the Stamp Act.

1767

June 29   **Townshend Acts**   Parliament passes the Townshend Acts, taxing glass, lead, paints, paper, and tea. The colonists boycott.

1768

October 1   British troops land in Boston to enforce the Townshend Acts. Tensions grow.

1770

March 5   **Boston Massacre**   British soldiers open fire on an angry Boston mob. Five colonists are killed.

In the wake of the killings, England withdraws her troops and repeals most of the taxes. They leave one tax in place—the tax on tea.

1773

November

Three ships with cargo holds full of tea sail into Boston Harbor.

December 16

Boston Tea Party   The Sons of Liberty, dressed as Mohawk Indians, dump the tea into Boston Harbor.

1774

April

Intolerable Acts   King George and parliament pass a series of acts to punish Boston.

May 27

British General Thomas Gage sails into Boston Harbor with four regiments of soldiers. All over Boston, church bells ring a funeral song to protest his arrival.

June 1

The Boston Port Bill, one of the "Intolerable Acts" goes into effect, closing Boston Harbor.

June 18

The Redcoats begin to strengthen the barricade at Boston Neck, cutting the city off from the rest of Massachusetts.

September 5

First Continental Congress   Representatives of twelve of the thirteen colonies (Georgia did not attend) meet in Philadelphia to discuss what to do about their problems with England.

--- **1775** ---

March 6   Dr. Joseph Warren delivers an address at Old South Meeting House to commemorate the fifth anniversary of the Boston Massacre.

March 20   Two British officers, disguised as colonials, map the road to Concord, Massachusetts, and identify the location of guns and gunpowder.

April 18   Redcoats assemble on Boston Common for a boat trip across the bay. Paul Revere begins his famous ride to warn the colonists in Lexington and Concord.

April 19   **Battles of Lexington and Concord**   Minutemen in Lexington and Concord turn out to meet the British troops. A shot is fired on Lexington Green and war breaks out. Patriots follow the British back to Boston and surround the city.

April 26   General Gage agrees to allow Patriots to leave Boston if they surrender their weapons and food.

May 10   **Second Continental Congress**   All thirteen colonies attend the second congress in Philadelphia to discuss the problems in Boston.

June 16	Under cover of darkness, the Patriots march to the top of Breed's Hill and build a fortification.
June 17	**The Battle of Bunker's Hill** The British suffer more than 1,100 casualties before a lack of gunpowder forces the Patriots to retreat. Dr. Joseph Warren is killed.
July 3	General George Washington arrives in Cambridge and takes command of the army.
August 3	Washington's troops have only 38 barrels of gunpowder. He sends spies into Boston to spread the rumor that he has 1,800 barrels.
August	The British chop down the Liberty Tree— a favorite meeting place of the Sons of Liberty.
October 4	Dr. Benjamin Church is convicted by a military council of being a spy for the British.
October 28	General Howe issues a proclamation stating that anyone caught leaving Boston without permission will be executed.

1776

January 1	General Washington raises a new flag on Prospect Hill, accompanied by a thirteen-gun salute. The flag has thirteen red and white stripes for the thirteen colonies, and the

British Union Jack in the upper left-hand corner.

January 9   Thomas Paine publishes a pamphlet called *Common Sense* urging the colonies to declare independence. It is an instant bestseller.

February 16   Washington's Council of War meets in Cambridge and decides to draw the British out of Boston by taking Dorchester Heights.

March 2   The Patriots begin the first of three nights of bombardments on Boston from Cobble Hill, Lechmere's Point, and Roxbury. On the third night, they climb to the top of Dorchester Heights and build a series of fortifications under cover of darkness.

March 5   At dawn the British discover that all of Washington's big guns are pointed right at them. A storm prevents a British attack.

March 17   British ships, filled with soldiers and Loyalists, leave Boston's wharves. The siege is over.

April 4   General Washington marches his army toward New York City.

July   A massive British war fleet arrives in New York Harbor, including 40,000 soldiers and sailors.

July 4	Congress approves the *Declaration of Independence.*
July 18	The Declaration reaches Boston and is read from the balcony of the Old State House.
August	The British win a number of battles in New York and New Jersey, forcing Washington's troops to retreat to Pennsylvania.
December 12	Concerned about a possible attack, the continental congress leaves Philadelphia for Baltimore.
December 25	**Battle of Trenton** Washington leads his troops across the Delaware River on Christmas night and successfully attacks British forces at Trenton, New Jersey, the next morning.

1777

October 7—17	**Second Battle of Saratoga** The British are defeated. Almost 6,000 Redcoats surrender. The news pushes France closer to forming a treaty with the new United States.
December 17	**Valley Forge** Washington's army encamps at Valley Forge, Pennsylvania, for the winter. One quarter of the army will die of starvation and sickness in the next six months.

1778

February	**France Enters the War**
December 29	The British capture Savannah, Georgia.

1779

January 29	The British capture Augusta, Georgia.
May 10	The British capture and burn Portsmouth and Norfolk, Virginia.

1780

May 6	**Siege of Charleston Ends** Charleston, South Carolina, falls to the British. It is the biggest American defeat of the entire war.
September 23	Washington's good friend Benedict Arnold is discovered to be a British spy. He escapes before he can be captured and is made a brigadier general in the British army.

1781

September 28	A force of Americans and French begin a siege of the British army at Yorktown, Virginia.
October 19	**Surrender at Yorktown** British General Charles Cornwallis surrenders.

1783

September 3	The Treaty of Paris formally ends the war.

★ GLOSSARY ★

Continental army: In June of 1775, after the war with England had begun, the Continental Congress adopted the New England army and formed the new Continental army, appointing George Washington its commander-in-chief.

Continental Congress: In 1774, each colony's legislature chose representatives to meet in Philadelphia and organize a protest to the Intolerable Acts. That was the First Continental Congress. In 1775, after the war broke out, the Second Continental Congress discussed independence and created the Continental army.

Intolerable Laws or Acts: Laws passed by the British to squash the American rebellion after the Boston Tea Party. They closed the port of Boston until the tea was paid for, changed the government of Massachusetts to bring it under the control of England, and required the colonists to house British soldiers in their own homes. Parliament called these laws the Coercive Acts because they were intended to coerce—or bully—the colonists into doing what England wanted. The colonists called the laws intolerable.

Lobsters: A slang term for a British soldier, because their coats were red as a lobster's shell.

Loyalist: An American who stayed loyal to King George. Loyalists were also called Tories.

militia: In America, an organized group of citizens who helped to defend their communities. Unlike regular soldiers who volunteered for the army, local militia groups promised to help in case of an emergency. Some members of the militia could be called upon at a moment's notice and were called Minutemen.

Minuteman: A Patriot ready to take up arms at a minute's notice.

New England army: The army that formed outside of Boston after the Battles of Lexington and Concord. It was called the New England army because most of the troops were from New England in the early days of the Boston siege.

parliament: The British parliament is the legislative arm of Great Britain's government—like our present-day Congress.

Patriot: Someone who loves his country. During the American Revolution, a colonist who supported the war of independence called himself a Patriot. The British called him a rebel.

Redcoat: A British soldier, so called because they wore red coats.

ringer: A marble game in which the marbles are placed in the middle of a circle. The point is to knock as many marbles out of the circle as possible using a larger, heavier marble called the shooter.

selectmen: The Board of Selectmen in Boston was the local government. They were elected by the people in town meetings. The Intolerable Acts, passed by the British Parliament, brought an end to town meetings unless they were approved by the royal governor.

siege: The act of surrounding a city or town, cutting it off from food and other supplies, to force it to surrender.

smallpox: A contagious disease that killed as many as forty out of one hundred people who caught it. People with smallpox broke out in painful pustules, or pox, that lasted for as long as a month. Those who survived the disease were often left with scars, or pock-marks.

Sons of Liberty: A secret group of American patriots that protested the taxes imposed by England. The first group probably formed in Boston, but they soon existed in almost every colony.

tyranny: A government in which a single leader has all the power and the people have no say in their own rule. When the British parliament passed the Intolerable Acts with King George's support, some Americans felt the parliament had acted illegally, ignoring their rights as Englishmen. These colonists believed they were living under tyranny, which they had a right to oppose.

★ FURTHER READING ★

Want to learn more about the American Revolution?
Here are some great nonfiction sources.

A Young Patriot: The American Revolution as Experienced by One Boy by Jim Murphy, published by Clarion Books, 1996. Joseph Plumb Martin enlisted in the army in 1776 at the age of fifteen. This book uses his diary to show us what life was like for one boy in the Continental army.

Fight for Freedom: The American Revolutionary War by Benson Bobrick, published by Atheneum, 2004. This is an excellent overview of the entire war with maps of some of the most important battles.

George Washington: An American Life by Laurie Calkhoven (yes that's me!), published by Sterling Publishing, 2006. Read about Washington's early experiences in the American wilderness, his role in the revolution, and his years as the nation's first president.

George Washington, Spymaster: How the Americans Outspied the British and Won the Revolutionary War by Thomas B. Allen, published by National Geographic, 2004. Washington's only hope of beating the British was to wage a war of spies and deception. This book is all about that secret world.

Give Me Liberty: The Story of the Declaration of Independence by Russell Freedman, published by Holiday House, 2000. This is an excellent look at the events leading up to the decision to declare independence and the personalities behind the famous document.

Acknowledgments

There truly are no words strong enough to express thanks for making a dream come true, but I'll try.

My heartfelt thanks go out to all of the wonderful people at Dutton who helped shepherd Daniel's story into print—Mark McVeigh, who started it all, along with Stephanie Owens Lurie, Steve Meltzer, Margaret Woollatt, and Rosanne Lauer.

I am so grateful to have so many good friends in my life who generously helped make this book a reality: Chris Dubois and Marjetta Geerling, the Thursday night champagne sisters (Josanne LaValley, Kekla Magoon, Connie Kirk, and Bethany Hegedus), and the Marcian Goddesses (Marnie Brooks, Marcia Thornton Jones, Martha Levine, Joanne Nicoll, Rebecca Rector, Susan Spain, and Barbara Underhill). Without their cheers, check-ins, critiques, and handholding, I never would have started, let alone finished.

John L. Bell did a fabulous job of pointing out where the facts in my story veered too far from the truth. Any errors that remain, of course, are mine.